CHATEAU DEBAUCHERY STARTER SET

Published by Em Brown
Copyright © 2017 by Em Brown

Printed in the USA.

Cover Design and Interior Format

Chateau DEBAUCHERY

Wicked Hot Erotic Romance

STARTER SET

Includes:

SUBMITTING TO LORD ROCKWELL

SUBMITTING TO THE RAKE

EM BROWN

For free ebooks, special promotions, and more wicked wantonness, visit:
www.EroticHistoricals.com

Table of Contents

A GENTLE WARNING

These stories contain BDSM elements, themes of submission and dominance, and many other forms of wicked wantonness.

Submitting TO LORD ROCKWELL

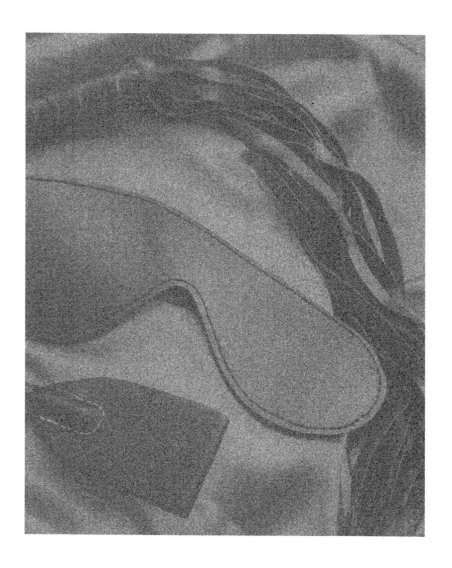

Chapter One

DEANA COULD MUSTER NO OATH strong enough to reflect the dismay she felt when Lord Halsten Rockwell revealed his ace and queen. She glanced at her own cards, a king and a ten, to ascertain she had indeed lost. How was it possible? Rockwell had been losing all night.

"You owe me fifty pounds, Miss Herwood," Lord Rockwell stated placidly as he collected the winnings in the middle of the table. It included a chit signed in her own hand.

She suppressed a glower, for she would not be dubbed bitter in defeat. It was evident from his immaculate dress—a perfectly tied cravat, a waistcoat sewn from the finest silk and a coat cut to fit his broad shoulders in tight embrace—that Rockwell had not her situation and was not in dire need of funds. She watched him replace a beautiful onyx ring upon his hand and found herself regarding his rugged fingers. She had never before paid much heed to a man's hand—or a woman's for that matter—but his conveyed strength, agility and even gentleness.

Dismissing the odd warmth that flared in her of a sudden, she glanced about the gaming hell for someone she might harry to lend her fifty quid. But the hour was late, the patrons at her table had left half an hour ago, and many of those remaining had debts themselves to pay. If only she had quit while ahead, but she had derived too much satisfaction from besting a man who possessed all that she did not—wealth, refined features and a quiet assurance that bordered on arrogance.

"I will repay you from my next winnings," she informed Rockwell.

"I have a better repayment option for you, Miss Herwood."

She raised her brows and waited patiently as he returned his purse to his coat. He looked across the card table at her. His dark-brown eyes reflected either the light of the candelabras or some inner merriment. His stare unsettled her, but not as much as what he said next.

"I would have you in my bed, Miss Herwood. For one night, I will take my pleasure of you, after which, your debt to me will be acquitted in its entirety."

"You would make of me a whore?" she asked when she had collected her wits and realized that he did not speak in jest. No one would mistake her family for members of the *ton*, but neither did her status merit such an affront.

"Let us have no pretentions, Miss Herwood. You relinquished your maidenhead years ago."

Her cheeks—nay, her entire countenance—flushed to know that he was privy to such confidence. Younger and more impulsive, she had surrendered her maidenhead to a man she thought would care for her. A colonel in His Majesty's Army, he was called to service before their affair could blossom into anything of consequence. Having lost her honor, she saw no reason subsequently not to indulge in the occasional affair, but she had always proceeded with great discretion. Her family had already suffered a fall from grace when she became a regular at the gaming hell, and she would not worsen the situation with more scandal.

Holding his gaze, she replied, "You overestimate the appeal of your company, Lord Rockwell. I would sooner double my obligation."

"Suit yourself," he said with dispassion and rose to his feet.

She considered how many hands of *vingt-et-un* she would have to win to secure fifty pounds and the litany of woes she would hear from her mother and aunt should she fail to bring home any income. They were a household of women since her father passed away, and the want of a man was never more palpable than now. If she could erase a debt of fifty pounds through one act—one night—might she be a fool to pass upon such an opportunity? As Lord Rockwell's barefaced assertion indicated, she no longer had any claim to a maiden's honor.

But what did she know of the man? Very little. He was not a frequent patron of her gaming hell. They had perhaps shared a card table once before; he had not taken much notice of her then. She, however, had not overlooked his presence, nor the women who threw themselves his way.

He possessed a countenance she would have enjoyed studying at length, much in the way one would admire a painting or sculpture. If he favored a lass here or there, it was difficult to ascertain, though surely no mortal could resist such attentions for long. Years ago, she had heard that banns would be read betwixt him and a Spanish princess or the daughter of a Duke or some such. Admittedly, the lack of a wedding ring was one of the first things she had noted when he sat down at her table this evening.

That he was always impeccably dressed also did not escape her, but many a man spent money he did not possess in order to maintain the appearance of wealth. She would not have allowed the wager to reach the sum of fifty pounds had she not felt assured of Lord Rockwell's finances. Unlike others, he did not flaunt his affluence. And though down by an even grander sum at one point, he showed no apprehension at the loss. How quickly thereafter the game had betrayed her!

Regardless of what she knew or thought of the man, her situation remained. If she did not accept his proposition, she was indebted to him for a significant amount of money. His demeanor suggested if she rebuffed him tonight, he would not necessarily renew his proposal.

"Pray, wait."

Lord Rockwell paused and looked down at her.

"I accept your offer," she informed him with eyes downcast. Honor or no, she could not look at him.

He inclined his head. "You honor me, Miss Herwood."

What a ridiculous statement, she thought, as if she had accepted an invitation for a ride in the park with him.

"There are rooms here reserved for more, er, amorous pursuits. Shall we retire to one of them?" she inquired, meeting his gaze this time, then wishing she hadn't. The contrast of dark intensity with the glimmer of light in his eyes disconcerted her.

"That won't do. The accommodations here are hardly adequate," he replied. "My carriage shall meet you here two nights hence. The wait will deepen the anticipation."

Anticipation? His or hers? Perhaps his self-assurance was arrogance after all.

"My only request," he continued with a stern tone, "is that you do not arrive inebriated."

Again, she reddened. She was known to have had a glass too many on occasion, but how did this man whom she barely knew acquire such knowledge of her? And why should it matter to him what state she was in? Lest he was expecting her to perform certain acts upon him? The thought made her blush deeper.

His features softened as he lifted her hand to his lips. "*Au revoir.*"

As she watched him depart, she began to regret her decision, for she could not attribute to indignation alone the warmth she felt spreading throughout her.

"**A**RE YOU HEADED TO THAT gaming hell again?" her aunt queried as Deana finished her supper and prepared to leave the table. "You'll never find a husband if you waste your hours there in the company of cads and rogues."

"Leave her be," her mother responded. "We can ill afford her not to go. It were not as if she had any marital prospects to entertain."

On that merry note, Deana ascended the stairs to her bedroom. Had she known her father would pass from an untimely failure of the heart, she would have sought matrimony earlier. While he had earned a decent income as a barrister, they had over time eaten into what savings they had, including funds intended as her dowry. If it were not for a flair and more luck than not at the card tables, she knew not how they would have fared. She had to acquit herself of her debt to Lord Rockwell or her hours at the gambling hall would be long indeed.

Struggling with her attire, she settled first on her plainest muslin, but vanity, and perhaps a subtle desire to please Lord Rockwell, led her to a simple but elegant gown of batiste. She could not deny a part of her was flattered that he wished to bed her. He had a physiognomy pleasing to the eye, a physique that knew few rivals, and a grace to his movements and carriage. She had relived the kiss to her hand over and over despite herself. The firmness, the gentleness with which he had held her hand and the deliberateness in how he had released her made her quiver. Though not uncomely herself, she would be as naïve as a schoolroom chit to think she was a skirt of singular interest to him. There were rumors enough of the women he had taken to bed, and undoubtedly others that had not risen to the level of tittle-tattle.

At the gaming hell, she drummed her fingers against the card table before bolstering her courage with a third glass of burgundy. She played a few rounds of faro, hoping that in the final minutes Lady Luck would spare her the humiliation of prostituting herself for a mislaid wager. She had assumed Lord Rockwell to be discreet, for she had not known him to confirm any of his *liaisons*, but she had no guarantee of his confidence. Granted, her patronage of a gaming hell had already diminished her repute, but word of her lifting her skirts to Lord Rockwell would discharge any prospects for matrimony—the only stable salvation for her family.

"Your carriage awaits, Miss Herwood," a footman informed her.

She retrieved her gloves and hat, pulling its veil low over her face before she stepped into the carriage. By the time it pulled up in front of Lord Rockwell's Town home, the burgundy had calmed her anxiety and put her in a more cheerful disposition. She had consumed three glasses of wine in the past with no significant impacts. Despite his command that she arrive sober, he would be no wiser. No doubt he differed little from others of his sex and, after twenty minutes, she would find him spent, her obligation complete, and herself returned home before midnight. Once inside, the butler offered to take her pelisse but she declined. He showed her into the drawing room. Compared to her address, the room was richly furnished and its décor stately but not garish. The gleam of the wood and the shine of the upholstery indicated the furnishings to be new or well cared for, unlike the few pieces her family owned or borrowed. A healthy fire kept the room warm and the candelabras on the silken walls gave it light. A small elephant carved from ivory caught her eye. She picked it up from the end table and admired the detailing and its two ruby eyes.

"Do sit, Miss Herwood."

She bobbled the figurine before clutching it tightly to her chest to keep it from falling. She turned in the direction of the rich tenor.

Lord Rockwell stood at the threshold, appearing as dapper in his banyan as he did in full dress. Quickly she returned the elephant to its home. The thought that she had nearly dropped what was no doubt an expensive item made her tremble. God knew what she would owe him then.

"Two and twenty thousand rupees," he answered. "It belonged to a Hindu rajah."

"It's beautiful," she murmured.

"Sit, Miss Herwood."

His imperial tone contrasted with the more courteous manners he exhibited at the gaming hell. Perhaps he fancied himself a rajah in his own abode. Though tempted to defy him, she sat down upon a settee, noting that tea had been set upon the table before it. He sat opposite her and poured her a cup, which she accepted gratefully, for she would not know what to do with her hands otherwise. She took a sip of the fragrant Darjeeling, ignoring his penetrating gaze.

"You're inebriated," he stated with a frown.

Damn. How the bloody hell did he discern that? Caught, she opted to mask her embarrassment with childish insolence.

"I had myself a glass," she admitted with a dismissive shrug, avoiding his stare by focusing on her tea. "I am no child, Lord Rockwell, and you are not my guardian."

"Indeed. If I were, you would certainly not be spending your time in a gaming hell."

"And if I were yours, you would not be making indecent propositions to ladies you hardly know."

His brows rose but his eyes glimmered with amusement.

"Such insolence can be tamed," he said almost to himself, then offered her the plate of biscuits. "You will require sustenance to soak up the effects of the wine."

She hesitated. The wine was giving her courage, but perhaps it was best she had all her wits about her with this man.

"The servants have all retired for the evening. You've no need to conceal yourself."

"You will forgive me if I fail to trust to assurances alone that our transaction, if you will, shall remain private."

After a moment of thought, he went to the writing table and retrieved paper and pen. After a quick scrawl, he affixed his seal and handed her the note.

"You may redeem this if the confidence of this night is broken," he told her.

She choked on her tea upon seeing the amount he had penned. Five hundred pounds!

"Do you make such offers to all the women you take to bed?" she could not help asking.

His expression darkened and she regretted her impudence.

"Consider yourself unique, Miss Herwood."

There was a peculiar strain to his voice. She took another sip of the tea to avoid his gaze. Of course the other women willingly lifted their skirts to him. She wondered if she would have done the same had she not lost to him.

"When do we, er, begin…?"

"Our 'transaction'?"

"Would you prefer a more romantic term?" she replied archly.

"Not at all. I have always observed you to be practical and devoid of the silly sensibilities and nonsense that permeate others of your sex."

He had observed her before? Should she be flattered by this? She began to wonder if he had deliberately chosen to sit at her card table the other night.

"We will conduct our matter when you are in full possession of your faculties," he continued, pouring her more tea, "that you may fully appreciate its aspects."

She could not help an unladylike snort. "You fancy yourself an accomplished lover, do you?"

He said nothing, but a smile tugged at the corner of his lips. They were a sensuous pair. For a moment, she wondered what it would feel like to be kissed by them. She shook herself back to attention, glad the veil shielded her, to a degree, from his discerning stare. The wine was having the damnable effect of making the man more attractive.

"I think you will find the experience agreeable, Miss Herwood."

"And how do you come to merit such arrogance?"

"You will discover for yourself soon enough."

She pursed her lips in frustration. She had hoped for a short visit and instead of concluding their business, they were having a *tête-à-tête* over bloody tea. Setting aside her cup, she untied her pelisse and allowed it to fall from her shoulders.

"Did you not wish to take your pleasure of me?"

A muscle along his jaw rippled as he settled further into the settee. "In due time."

Tiresome man.

Those with wealth and countenance assumed the world revolved about them. A rush of envy stoked a darker side of her. In the end he was but a man, with base desires no different than a commoner, and she would prove it so. She unpinned her hat and fixed her most smoldering stare upon him. She had witnessed the coquetry of the women who patronized the gaming hell and been entertained by how simply a man could be lured into their grasps.

"Have you ever considered becoming a courtesan to relieve your fiscal conditions?"

His uncanny ability to know her thoughts unnerved her, and the truth of the matter struck a vulnerable chord. She had considered the option but simply had no prospects at the moment.

"If you are offering, Lord Rockwell, I am flattered but must decline," she retorted as she removed her gloves, slowly peeling one past her elbow and exposing the smooth, pale skin of her forearm.

The corner of his mouth quirked upward. They both knew he had no intention of inviting her to be his mistress, but her response amused him. His gaze fell to her bare arms. The heat in his eyes made her feel as if she had taken off all her garments, not just her gloves. Emboldened by his appreciation, she angled herself on the settee and put a hand to the nape of her neck.

"I seem to have missed a pin," she said. "Would my lord oblige in removing it?"

He made no movement, making her wonder whether her inexperience in playing the coquette appeared that obvious, but then he crossed the distance between them and sat down beside her, his thigh dangerously close to her rump. She felt his fingers upon her hair and suppressed a shiver.

"You are mistaken, Miss Herwood. I see none."

She could sense the warmth of his body, and when he trailed a knuckle down the length of her neck, she suddenly wanted him to grab her and kiss her. But he had resumed his seat opposite her, leaving her wanting. She frowned. *He* had propositioned *her*. Did he expect that *she* would throw herself at *him*? Looking into his eyes, she suspected that he knew the effect he had on her. But she must have impressed him to some degree or he would not have offered to forfeit fifty pounds for one night of attention. Granted, fifty pounds was no significant sum for him, but he could have had women of far more consequence at his beck and call for far less.

Inspired by this reasoning, she stood up and sauntered toward him.

"Shall we retire to your bedchamber, my lord?"

"I prefer different quarters."

His response struck her as odd, but the sofa upon which he sat appeared comfortable enough. She dropped to her knees, the wine humming in her veins. Surprise lighted his eyes but he did not move. His gaze caressed the swell of her cheek, the skin above her décolletage and, seeming to penetrate the material of her dress, the curves beneath. Her body tingled from head to toe beneath his regard. She dared to put a hand upon his knee. When he did not flinch, she glanced into his countenance and thought she saw flames in his eyes.

"You have managed to learn the arts of a courtesan," he observed coolly, with only the faintest hitch in his voice.

Her heart hammered in her ears. She was a novice playing with fire. Never before had she been so bold with a man. But never before had she dealt with a man who refused to be seduced by the very woman he had propositioned.

"You have finished neither your biscuit nor your tea, Miss Herwood."

"I have no need for your tea and biscuit. I am in full command of my faculties, Lord Rockwell, despite the presence of a bit of wine," she responded.

"Ah, Miss Herwood, how poorly you lie."

She would have risen, thrown her hands up in exasperation and reached for her gloves and hat, daring him to stop her from leaving, but he had cupped her chin in one hand, his forefinger lazily grazing the soft spot beneath her jaw. She fought the desire to melt into his hand and the weakening in her limbs, for she had to uphold her earlier assertion. It was no easy battle, and the wine, which had hitherto been her supporter, turned foe in this matter.

"You contravened my command. I would have overlooked one glass of wine, but you have partaken of more, Miss Herwood."

Command? The word jolted her to attention and she pulled away from him. His touch rattled her senses far too much.

"You insist upon playing my guardian, Lord Rockewell?"

He smiled. "If that were the case, you would be splayed across my lap for a sound spanking."

Her mouth went dry at the thought. A small voice inside advised her to run from this man. At the very least she ought to put some distance between them, but a darker side of her was drawn to him more than ever.

"Patience, my dear Miss Herwood," he gently coaxed.

Patience? Would he have her return to her seat, twiddle with the damn biscuits and wait…wait for what?

"Have I misunderstood your proposition, Lord Rockwell? Did you not say that I could discharge my debt if I were to lay with you?"

"I did proffer one night of pleasure."

"And by pleasure you meant a *tête-à-tête* over tea? La! How silly of me to have suspected you of more roguish intentions."

As she spoke, she realized a part of her would be quite disappointed if he answered in the affirmative. She rose to her feet but he grabbed her at the wrist and pulled her across him with startling deftness. How easily he manhandled her.

"Make no mistake, Miss Herwood. I intend to take my pleasure of you," he growled, his mouth beside her ear.

"Then why delay, my lord?" she whispered back against his ear over the loud thumping of her heart.

He made a low groan. Before she could react, he had pinned her against the arm of the sofa. His mouth was atop hers, crushing, claiming, punishing. She had never been kissed with such force and felt a surge of triumph. Her head swam from the heady combination of intoxication and arousal. She attempted to return his forceful kiss, but his mouth dictated the terms. He tasted of her, explored her, consumed her. She could do little but surrender to his attentions.

When at last he released her to breathe, and the world had slowed its swirl about her head, she could not resist saying, "Patience, my lord."

"Patience be damned," he returned, though the glint in his eye had her suspecting that perhaps her triumph was not as complete as she would think. What was he concealing from her?

Chapter Two

SHE DID NOT DWELL LONG for he captured her mouth once more in his and she was content to revel in his desire for her. He trailed his lips down her neck and her back arched of its own volition, pressing her body into his, feeling the weight of him. She had not expected that area to prove so sensitive. As if cognizant of that delicacy, he kissed her with feathery lightness, a contrast to the vehemence with which he had plumbed her mouth earlier. His hand went to the small of her back, and that too proved provocative. She felt surrounded by him.

Desire swelled below her waist. She put her hand to the back of his neck, brushing the ends of his hair as he nestled into her neck. Forgetting her intentions to make quick her obligation to him, she allowed him to take his time caressing her décolletage and skimming the tops of her breasts. She had expected him to ravish them. In her previous encounters, the men had torn at her bodice as if they were starving babes eager to nurse, but she sensed that Lord Rockwell was no callow lover. Her nipples hardened, desiring his attention. As if sensing her precise need, he cupped a breast and grazed the nipple with his thumb. Her breath caught as a jolt of sensation shot from her nipple to the apex of her thighs. His thumb circled the nipple, rubbing the fabric of her dress into the bud until she squirmed and moaned her need for release.

He slid his hand to her upper thigh. Would he now throw up

her skirts and mount her? She found she did not dread the prospect. Indeed, the carnal yearning within her welcomed it. But instead of unbuttoning his trousers, he pulled up the hem of her dress and ran his hand along her leg. How she wished she had a better pair of stockings to present to a man who undoubtedly knew all the luxuries in life. He brushed the soft skin just above the stockings with his knuckles, his hand dangerously close to where her desire pooled hot and wet.

She glanced into his face. His soft brown eyes gleamed in a manner that made her reconsider once more the wisdom of her intoxication. He had the upper hand in more ways than one. But she had no time to chide herself for his fingers skimmed the patch of hair at the base of her pelvis. His thumb slipped lower and teased that small but potent nub of flesh between her legs. She closed her eyes against his stare, marveling at the delicious disconcertion in her body. Lightly he fondled her clitoris, nipped it between two fingers, stroked its length 'til she was panting. Her body, now a coil that needed unwinding , strained to his touch. In response he deepened his caress. Dipping a finger into her hot wetness, he rubbed her with increasing vigor.

Gasping, she felt herself thrown over a familiar precipice, only it felt more glorious than when she attended to her needs in solitude. She erupted in uncontrolled paroxysms against him. A cry escaped her lips. He pushed the last of the spasms from her body before easing his caress into a gentle swirling. She shuddered.

"You spend beautifully, Miss Herwood."

She barely heard his words. Lost in a fog of relief and glory and the remnants of her inebriation, she allowed herself to sink into the sofa. If he wanted her to attend him, he would have to wait and acquire some of the patience he had advocated earlier.

DEANA FLUTTERED HER EYES. SETTLED in a haze of comfort and satisfaction, she had no desire to move, but the aroma of fresh coffee called to her. She glanced down at the luxurious blanket covering her legs and felt the firm cushions beneath her. Her gaze moved to the porcelain coffee set in front of her and then across the table to the opposite sofa where Lord Rockwell sat, one leg crossed over the other, his expression soft.

Good heavens, had she fallen asleep?

Quickly she sat up, but the speed of her motions made the side of her head throb.

"Coffee will aid your situation," he offered, pouring a cup.

Flushing, she took the hot beverage with gratitude. He was correct—she should not have come intoxicated. She noticed he was no longer wearing his banyan or any neckwear. Instead, the top buttons of his shirt were undone—a minor feature but grandly provocative. Memories of what had transpired betwixt them rushed into her mind, warming her body instantly.

"Forgive my impoliteness for having, er, fallen asleep on your settee," she said more to her coffee than to him. She had never fallen asleep in a strange place before.

"I am glad for it," he replied. "Do you drink often, Miss Herwood?"

She eyed him carefully. "You seem to know much about me. Do you not already have your answer, your lordship?"

"A gaming hell is no place for one of the fair sex to let down her guard."

"I am no fool nor child."

"Tonight being the exception?"

She tried not to glare at him. "Though I am sure you are accustomed to women throwing themselves at you, might you allow that one would deem the situation I find myself facing rather daunting?"

His lips curved in genuine humor and she found it hard to remain angry with him. How glorious those lips had felt upon her...

"Miss Herwood?"

Realizing she had been staring at his mouth, she buried her face in her coffee. What a gauche young woman he must perceive her to be!

"Please partake of the sweatmeats." He gestured to the berries, cheese and bread on the coffee tray.

Though not particularly hungry, she decided to eat as a distraction and idly wondered if he had woken the servants in the middle of the night to prepare the coffee.

He poured himself a cup and settled back into the sofa to gaze upon her. She wanted to quip about the impoliteness of staring, but the entitled would not care for comments from one such as her. Instead, she broke the silence with small talk.

"Do you travel to India often?"

"What do you consider often? It is no easy journey."

She had no definition in mind. The farthest she had ever been from London was Bath.

"Would you venture there if it were not?" she rephrased.

He weighed her query. "In truth, I am ambivalent. There is much to wonder at and detest of the East."

She tried to fathom a world she had seen only in books and an occasional painting, but in her mind danced colorful silks, teas and curries.

"Tell me of India."

"Many would find her easy to disdain, but you would appreciate India."

"You know me well enough to make such a declaration?"

"I merely observe the inflection when you speak and the shine in your eyes. You are not difficult to read, Miss Herwood."

She frowned. She was gauche *and* guileless?

"Do not distress yourself. Consider it a compliment. I find it refreshing."

Is that what had attracted him to her table?

"I imagine a visitor from India could find much to disdain in England," she remarked. "For instance, certain noblemen can be quite insufferable here."

He grinned at her taunt. "I couldn't agree more, Miss Herwood. More coffee?"

She eagerly accepted, for the coffee did aid with her headache and she was beginning to enjoy her conversation with Lord Rockwell.

"I think you are partial to India, Lord Rockwell."

"Indeed?"

She gestured about the room. "You have reminders of her everywhere."

He followed her gaze from the elephant she had held earlier to a bronze oil lamp above the fireplace to a tapestry on the wall. The image on the tapestry was a woman wearing a golden head-dress, arms stretched with a bow and arrow, astride a many-hued parrot.

"Rati," he explained. "Hindu goddess of love, passion and carnal pleasure."

Her cheeks colored. She recalled her purpose for being here and, as she had pointed out earlier, it was not for conversation.

"How appropriate," she murmured. "I am aware that I have not fulfilled my end of the arrangement, my lord."

"Not entirely. I took great pleasure in seeing you spend."

Her whole body flushed. She shifted under his gaze.

The fires in his eyes flared. "I have much more planned, Miss Herwood."

She swallowed with difficulty the coffee she had just imbibed and felt a strong need to fan herself.

"How do you wish to begin?" she croaked.

"Come here," he said, his tone gentle and commanding.

She went to stand before his sofa. He rose to his feet. Looking down at her, he brushed a stray tendril of hair over her shoulder.

"What does your body desire most, Miss Herwood?" he asked.

You. At that moment, she realized that she had never desired a man as much as she did then. The embers from his recent caresses were quick to burn anew.

"My lord?"

"What brings you the greatest pleasure?" He slid the back of his forefinger down her neck and along her collarbone.

"Having a romp at the tables against haughty noblemen."

He circled his arm around her waist and jerked her to him. She could feel his hardened cock against her hip.

"I promise you will enjoy having lost to me, Miss Herwood." As he held her against him, his other hand cupped her jaw and lifted her face. "You shall not soon forget this night."

"And what have I done to merit such a prospect?" she asked quietly, momentarily mesmerized by the depths of his eyes. Like diamonds, they reflected an inner fire.

His thumb passed over her mouth, tugging the bottom lip down. He grazed the tip of her tongue. She caught his thumb in her mouth and sucked. Hard.

He groaned. Removing his thumb, he replaced it with his mouth. She could taste the coffee and, beyond that, him. His mouth covered hers, his tongue probed and coaxed. Her head was spinning, she had never experienced such a full and luscious kiss. Deeper he went but in steps that assured she could follow. Not at all like her last lover, who harkened to her mind a pet dog she once had. The dear little bitch would greet her with all tongue, lapping at her face and drowning her in slaver.

Lord Rockwell's kiss was consuming but purposeful. His lips led hers in a heady dance that left her breathless and wanting. His cock felt like a steel rod against her. She pressed her hips to him, the carnal yearning in her body needing to connect with his. He responded by gripping her tighter, one hand cupping a buttock so that she remained molded to him. She let out a small gasp. He dropped his head and tongued the hollow of her neck. Any lingering regrets of having lost to Lord Rockwell at the card table vanished. She wanted him to take her and satiate the burning within her. Wrapping her arms around his neck, she pulled him into her. She would be content to kiss for an eternity but for the ache building within her. Her hand slid from his neck to the slight opening of his shirt.

Abruptly he whipped her around and pinned her backside against him. The thickness of his desire pressed against her derriere. One arm circled her chest, the other her pelvis. She could have melted into his embrace. As he rained kisses along her neck, he groped a breast, kneading the flesh through her dress. Her nipple puckered beneath his touch. She wanted his other hand to pull up her skirts as he had done and fondle once more that most sensitive of parts.

"Select a word," he murmured as he nipped her earlobe.

"Pardon?"

"A word that when uttered will halt whatever I do."

She pondered the reason behind the peculiar request as Rati looked down upon them through half-lidded eyes.

"My lord?"

He brushed aside the stray strands of hair at her nape and sucked upon her neck. "Select a word and you shall understand soon enough."

She noticed a faint smile upon the Hindu goddess. "Rati."

"I like your choice, Miss Herwood."

He pulled away from her. She looked at him, disappointed. Had she not complied?

Taking her by the hand, he led across the drawing room and, pulling a key from his pocket, unlocked a door she had not noticed before.

The room she entered was dark but for two bronze oil lamps on either side of what appeared to be a low sleeping area comprised of large plush pillows, a blood-red canopy with golden tassles and orange silk curtains. It was beautiful, fit for an Indian princess. But as she widened her view, she saw in the corner of the room a mattress adorned with only a stark white sheet. The headboard was made of iron bars like those found in a gaol. On the wall hung more implements one might find in a gaol or medieval dungeon—crops, whips, shackles and ropes.

"Do not fear," Rockwell said. "All that you see is intended for your pleasure."

"Pleasure?" she echoed in disbelief. "Are these the teachings of Rati?"

"No. For the sinful delights of flogging, one need look no further than *Fanny Hill*."

She flushed at the thought and began to wonder if she needed to flee.

"I presume you have never been flogged for pleasure, Miss Herwood."

"I have never been flogged for pleasure or otherwise," she protested.

"We may or may not have the opportunity tonight."

Her eyes widened. "Your proposition made no mention of such…errant…"

"You asked for no specifics."

"What woman of sound mind could have guessed—"

"I stated that I would take my pleasure of you. I promise that you too will enjoy every moment."

He spoke without hauteur and she was tempted to believe the sincerity in his tone. Needing some distance from him to process her thoughts, she walked over to one wall and inspected a cat-o'-nine-tails. She touched the leather tails. It was real and no mere plaything.

"You have used this on other women?" she inquired.

He walked up behind her. She tensed. His presence alone could send her judgment scattering. Already her body responded as if being called by sirens.

"I have," he replied.

"And they did not dislike it?"

"Quite the contrary."

She closed her eyes at his seductive voice. She wanted to trust him.

"Surely you can forgive my skepticism," she resisted.

"Have I not attended you with satisfaction?"

He ran a finger up her bare arm and she could not quell a shiver. How had her body become so sensitized to his touch?

"What you require is beyond the norm," she murmured.

He rested his hand upon her shoulder, then gently began rubbing away the tension.

"I would not have invited you here if I did not think you possessed a bold spirit. I shall do nothing you cannot bear. You have but to utter your chosen word."

"Rati."

"Precisely. You may invoke it at any time. I would not have provided you this safety if I meant to force my will upon you. All that I do is for your desire."

She raised a brow. "I will desire you to flog me?"

The corner of his mouth curled upward. "You will."

"I very much doubt it, my lord."

His eyes glimmered. "Care to lay wager upon it, Miss Herwood?"

"Despite my conviction, I think I had best not."

"Then to allay your fears, allow me to propose that if you do not find this night to be fulfilling, I will offer as recompense the sum of one hundred pounds."

A hundred quid! She salivated at the sum. She could stall the creditors from repossessing the furniture. Her mother could indulge in jam and butter upon her toast.

"And how would you define fulfillment?"

He trailed his hand down to the swell of her breast. "Not I. You shall—with your orgasm. The absence of it would mark a night unfulfilled."

She gazed down at his hand. One hundred pounds. And she had but to refrain from spending?

"You mock me, Lord Rockwell."

"I rarely jest on such matters."

His hand dipped beneath her décolletage and cradled a breast. She closed her eyes. His touch was exquisite.

"Do you make a habit of such outrageous propositions?"

"Would you believe me if I said I did not?"

"No."

He kissed her lightly upon the neck. "Then why ask?"

She sighed. Exasperating if not clever man.

He whipped her around and pressed his mouth full upon hers.

"Come, I dare you to accept the wager," he murmured against her lips.

Chapter Three

THE WARMTH BETWEEN HER LEGS flared once more, but she forced her mind to the task. "You have me at a disadvantage. I have but your word that you will honor both the word of safety and your wager."

He pulled back and stared deep into her eyes. "Your dilemma is understandable. I can only ask that you trust me."

Her heart throbbed with excitement and fear. Thriving in a gaming hell necessitated the constant assessment of character, and her instincts gave no alarm with Lord Rockwell. She wanted to place herself in his hands, but she barely knew the man. And yet she had never felt more at ease in a man's company.

A hundred pounds. It was too grand a sum not to take the risk. "Very well, Lord Rockwell, I accept."

His smile reached his eyes and she sensed her relief reflected also in him.

"I promise you will not rue the hand you lost at *vingt-et-un*."

He led her to a mirror and stood once more behind her. It was most disconcerting for she knew not what he would do, nor could she read his countenance.

"Tell me what arouses you," he instructed as his hand brushed the skin above the back of her bodice.

"You are most forward, Lord Rockwell, and I have no intention of giving you any assistance in winning your wager."

She saw his smile in the mirror.

"Touché. I will discern the answer nonetheless."

He began to unbutton her gown.

Dialogue could prove a good distraction, she decided. "How many women have you entertained in this chamber of yours?"

The answer should dampen her lust.

"You are most forward, Miss Herwood."

She could not help a grin at his response.

"I have not kept count."

"Several?"

"Define 'several'."

He eased the top of her gown down her arms. It pooled at her feet. She watched in the mirror as he untied her petticoats next.

"Four or more?"

"Or more, certainly."

The petticoats fell to the ground. She blushed at the sight of herself in chemise and corset. He began to unlace her corset without effort.

"Should not a man of your stature be seeking a wife instead of indulging in prurient interests?" she asked, averting her eyes from the mirror.

"Should not a woman of your situation be seeking a husband instead of gambling at a gaming hell?" he returned.

She bristled. "I asked first."

"A wife is easy enough to attain. I see no reason to rush."

How she wished she could claim the same of a husband!

"I am earning my dowry, if you will, at the gaming hell."

Clever response, she praised herself.

"You require a husband with funds, not a man in search of a dowry."

She pursed her lips at his obvious statement, which made quick work of her smugness.

"It is no easy matter to find a man with funds and possessing a decent character."

"Especially in a gaming hell."

Their dialogue was proving quite effective, for now anger

trumped all that she felt. To her surprise, tears threatened. She was well aware that her current finances necessitated her spending time in a gaming hell, which dimmed her marital prospects and future security.

"You see the irony of my situation then," she replied with an edge. "I have not the fortune to have been born into the *ton* or with a bounty of assets at my disposal."

The corset dropped from her.

"I beg to differ," Rockwell said.

She saw herself wearing only her chemise, stockings and garters.

He slid the sleeve of the chemise down a shoulder and kissed her there. "You have remarkable assets."

He gripped the flimsy fabric and tore it in twain down the front, exposing her breasts, her abdomen, her pelvis. She gasped and stared at the mirror in shock. Modesty finally set in and she looked away. As if his words had not riled her enough, he had to destroy her chemise as well?

"I will compensate you for your loss, but look in the mirror, Deana."

She should chastise him for the familiar use of her name, but she fixed her concentration upon the ground.

"Look," he ordered in a tone she found difficult to disobey.

She moved her gaze to the mirror.

"You are lovely."

He pulled the torn garment from her and circled his arms around to cup her breasts.

"In addition to many other fine attributes in your possession," he continued.

He tugged at her nipples and all her anger dissipated, replaced with a poignant need. She looked away once more, but he took her chin and directed her to the mirror.

"Look at yourself," he commanded.

She raised her eyes.

"I am no poet," he said, "or I could speak eloquently of these."

Once more he fondled her breasts. Desire warmed in her loins despite the awkwardness of having to look upon her own nakedness.

"And these."

His hands dropped to her hips.

"And this."

One hand reached the triangle of hair at her groin. How delicious his warm, strong hands felt upon her body…

A hundred pounds, she reminded herself.

"You have the body of a goddess."

His voice was a caress as powerful as his touch.

"That of lithe Artemis," he continued, "or Athena."

He took both her hands in his and guided them to her breasts and over her belly. He moved their right hands between her thighs. She gasped. She was touching herself in front of him! He stroked her flesh through her fingers. His left hand moved hers back to a breast, palming the mound, rolling it over her chest. She needed to escape the assault of sensations but tried not to squirm. He began strumming against her flesh, bumping her fingers into herself. She squeezed her thighs together to limit the movements but he managed to push her forefinger into her wet, hot cunnie.

Dear God, he's making me frig myself. She was both aroused and flustered. He lifted his head to see her countenance. The flash in his eyes made her heart thump even more. He pushed her finger deeper inside her while he pressed his thumb upon her clit. Gradually he increased the motions of both hands. Her head fell against his shoulder at the onslaught. She could look no more. Wonderful sensations brewed and ricocheted inside her.

A hundred pounds. A hundred pounds. A hundred pounds.

"Do not move," he said, withdrawing his hands.

She saw herself in the mirror, one hand upon her breast, the other buried between her legs. Her cunnie throbbed around her finger. When he stepped away to retrieve something, she pulled out of herself and covered herself.

"You moved," he scolded upon his return.

The darkness of his tone quickened her pulse. A threat lay beneath his words. She saw he held a long thick rope. He planted a simple wooden chair behind her.

"And I have yet to punish you, Miss Herwood, for your first indiscretion."

Punish?

"My lord?"

"I specifically told you not to come inebriated."

She felt like a chastened child but retorted, "I forget you are accustomed to women doing all that you bid."

He pulled the rope taut between his hands. "By all means, contravene me at every turn. I take as much delight in administering punishment as I do pleasure. Arms behind you, please."

After a brief hesitation, she complied, praying that she would not regret her decision to place all trust in him. With the servants asleep, there would be no one to come to her rescue should she need it. She doubted they would hear her screams through the door and down into the servants' quarters.

Standing in front of her, Rockwell looped the rope around her neck, crossed it in front of her chest and wound one end beneath a breast, around her arms in back, under the other breast and back up to her neck. He did the same in mirror fashion with the other end. With the skill of a weaver, he wrapped the rope about her 'til her arms were pinioned and her breasts trapped, simultaneously propped up by the rope beneath and pressed down from the rope above. He bent her arms at the elbows and tied her forearms together. He stepped back to evaluate his handiwork.

The sight of herself in the mirror, her stockings and garters still upon her, her bosom bound, was unexpectedly *beautiful*.

"Did you learn this in India?" she asked, liking the look and feel of her body in the rope. Its rough dryness contrasted with the soft suppleness of her skin.

"It is a Japanese art form. Do you remember your safety word?"

She nodded.

"Speak it."

"Rati."

"Good."

He held one of her protruding breasts, then let it go and slapped its underside. She gasped, mostly in surprise. His hand came down upon the top of it. The thick flesh, confined by the rope, jiggled once. She could hardly believe that he had struck her, yet the contrast of that touch with the tenderness of his earlier caresses was invigorating. He spanked the other breast, a little harder this time, but she did not recoil. She looked at him to see that he was appraising her responses.

"Do you require your safety word, Miss Herwood?"

"No."

She wanted him to continue his attentions. He obliged, slapping one breast then the other. Her cunnie pulsed. Not only could she bear the punishment, it had the surprising effect of arousing her further. Gripping the rope around her chest, he pulled her to her feet. Her gaze caught in his, she sensed she could have been prey he intended to devour. His mouth plunged down upon hers. She could do nothing but submit to his ferocious kiss and understood then why he had wanted her sober—that she could appreciate every maddening sensation, be it pleasant or painful or a strange mixture of both. When he released her from his kiss, she felt as if a fine wine had been dashed from her lips. She wanted more, wanted his tongue to continue probing her depths.

He repositioned the chair in front of her and bent her over the back of it. In the mirror she saw a woman, naked, her chest bound in rope, her posterior protruding before his lordship. What a wanton wench was this woman staring back at her!

"What implement do you favor for your punishment—the crop, whip, or—?"

"I favor none."

"Ah, shall we try them all then?"

"The nine-tails."

She hoped that she had selected the right instrument. The wide leather tapes of the nine-tails looked less imposing than the crop or single whip, both of which would no doubt sting. As she watched him remove the implement of choice from the wall, she assuaged her fear by telling herself that the pain would no doubt dampen all arousal and thus allow her to win the wager.

Upon his return, he caressed the curve of her rump and grasped a handful of the flesh. She closed her eyes. Never had she been so exposed to a man, her most private of parts manhandled in such a manner.

Releasing her arse, he gave it a pat. "You are quite delectable, Miss Herwood. Do you recall your safety word?"

Would she need it?

"Yes, my lord."

His hand slipped past her buttocks to the wetness between her legs. She groaned. He teased and tormented that traitorous nub of desire. Despite her efforts to resist, she felt the arousal intensifying, felt herself growing hotter and wetter. She shifted, both from having to hold herself up against the discomfort of the hard chair and the ache emanating from within.

"Please," she mumbled.

"Miss Herwood?"

"Please...punish me."

Silence.

Was he reveling in his victory? Did he intend to emphasize his earlier prediction by making her beg even more? Glancing in the mirror, she saw the bulge at his crotch. Perhaps she was not the only one fighting back urges.

He stepped back and splayed the tails against a buttock. She gasped. As she had hoped, the tails landed with a thud and not a sting. He backhanded her other buttock with the flogger, warming her skin and making it tingle. The next blow landed with greater force, but not much worse than the spanking her breasts had received at his hand. She wondered how much of his full strength he would employ. Though her heartbeat quickened at the question, she felt she could trust him not to harm her. The tails slapped against her derriere in varying rhythms, warming her whole body, invigorating it. Even the blows that made her wince and grunt proved enlivening. Her bottom ached, but every nerve had come alive. When he paused and ran his hand between her legs, she nearly fell off the chair.

Dear God. Shutting her eyes, she concentrated on staying in place, pretending the exquisite sensations at her quim were not hers. She was elsewhere. This woman at the mercy of Lord Rockwell, this woman bound and flogged was not her. *Think of something inane!*

Her mind went briefly to her aunts recounting their walks through Hyde Park, whom they saw, what was worn by those they saw, whom they didn't see…

Something else rubbed at her cunnie—the flogger! She groaned as the tails moved against her, brushing her most intimate parts.

Abruptly he pulled the flogger back and lashed its tips upon her buttocks. This time it stung, but his earlier ministrations had overwhelmed her and the pain served only to make her crave his touch even more. He began a wicked dance between flogging her arse and caressing her quim. Any control her mind had on the situation was fast slipping away under the onslaught of sensations.

"Ahhh!" she cried after one particularly hard blow.

He stroked her aching cunnie, stoking the tension in her loins. Lubricated by her wetness, his hand created a delicious friction against her. She could not ignore the heat engulfing her body, the blood pumping in her veins. The odds of her winning the hundred quid were no longer in her favor. Her body craved to be led up to the precipice over which she would find release.

No! She wanted him to cease. Should she employ her word of safety? For his caresses? Nay, she was no weakling…though her legs were beginning to weaken under the strain. Best to bring an end to this and find relief in that grandest of carnal ecstasies…

He returned to the flogger and slapped it across her arse. She cried out once again. Not only did it hurt, but she was painfully aware of the absence of his fondling. The sound of leather against flesh filled the chamber along with her cries and groans. She began to doubt how much more she could withstand. Doubtless the hundred pounds would not apply if she were to use the safety word.

"Still yourself," he growled when she shifted her weight. "You will not want for the tails to land outside their target."

Oddly, his command reassured her. She braced herself and withstood the next two blows. Her body had never felt more alive. Her arse burned alongside a carnal heat, one fueling the other, both consuming. He whipped the tails against her bottom, making the flesh quiver. She rather hoped he would reward her with more caresses.

Or did she? She cursed to herself. *A hundred pounds...*

As she warred with herself, Rockwell grasped her hair and pulled her into a standing position. He cast aside the flogger, walked her to the sumptuous bedding and pushed her to her knees. He bent her over a stack of pillows. The softness was a grateful contrast to the chair. A silky plume swept over her rump. The simple feather could have ignited her highly sensitized buttocks. She shivered and tried not to notice how her wetness was running down her thighs.

She heard the rustle of his clothes being shed and remembered how inviting his chest had looked beneath his unbuttoned shirt. Twisting her head, she looked behind herself to see his cock spring from his pants. Thick and hard, it was a beautiful member. She wanted it, needed it to tame the heat inside her.

No, that will not do! She needed to prevail with this wager. She forced her mind to consider the soreness in her arms, the tenderness of her derriere, the humiliation of being trussed up before this man, her most intimate parts fully exposed and at his mercy.

"What a lovely blush adorns your arse," he admired of his handiwork.

And yet there was something quite titillating, exhilarating and seductive in submitting to Lord Rockwell.

He encased his cock with a protective sheath. Partaking of her wetness, he rubbed it upon the covering and looked at her. The dark hunger in his eyes made her cunnie throb. She straightened her head and took a deep breath. When his cock grazed her, she gasped in delight. He sawed his erection between her legs. Back and forth. Back and forth. As pleasurable as the action was, she wanted more.

Take me, she nearly shouted.

As if reading her mind, he plunged himself into her. Her cunnie clutched at his cock greedily. How marvelous he felt inside her. She would have savored the sensation longer but her arousal, brought to a famished height, was impatient for more. Her hips moved of their own volition. He moved his own in rhythm to hers until he was thrusting deeper and deeper into her. She moaned her appreciation. *Yes...*

No.

She managed to calm her hips. With her mind she tried to extinguish the fire consuming her. The effort made her feel as if her body would twist itself inside out.

He reached around her and pinched a nipple. The sensation shot straight to her cunnie. He continued his thrusting and gently slapped a buttock. He groped the orb, his large hand covering her flesh. She had never thought such attentions to her arse would prove so provocative. He circled his hand around her hip for her clitoris, stroking the engorged nub as he pumped his cock in and out of her.

No, no, no...yes...no...yes!

Desire vibrated with unbearable intensity within her. The tide pushed against her now meager wall of resistance and her body shattered into a thousand pieces. She cried out as the waves washed over her. Spasms rippled through her limbs, jerking her against him. She vaguely heard him grunt and felt his thrusts quicken before he fell atop her, his weight pushing her into the pillows. They lay, their bodies still joined, taking in air as they sank back to earth.

A FULL SENNIGHT HAD PASSED SINCE her visit with Lord Rockwell and still her cheeks flushed when she recalled their assignation. For days she could not sit without feeling the flogger upon her arse.

Applying a balm to the affected area, he had murmured, "Well done, Miss Herwood."

Despite having lost the wager, she had felt quite satisfied with herself. She had not required her safety word. Her body had been pushed to limits she had never thought possible. The whole experience had been *unworldly*.

With tenderness, he had removed her bonds and rubbed her sore arms as she lay against him, her body spent. And that too proved pleasurable. She would have been content to fall asleep in his arms but for the need to return before the household awoke. He had attended to her toilette with the air of a gentleman, notwithstanding what he had just done to her.

"I presume my debt to be disposed of?" she had inquired before departing.

His eyes had glimmered. "Indeed."

"Then I bid you good evening—or good day, rather."

"Good day, Miss Herwood."

He had lifted her hand to his lips. The kiss had sent the embers of desire flaring and she would have been tempted to stay if he had asked her to.

"Oh that I could have a new ribbon for my bonnet. This one has lost its color and is more white than pink."

Her aunt's voice broke into her reverie.

Deana studied the petticoat she was mending for the fourth time. Perhaps she should have tried harder to win the hundred pounds from Lord Rockwell. She would not have minded another hand at cards with the man—and she was unsure whether she would prefer to win or lose against him.

She looked outside the drawing room window at the setting sun. It was almost the time when she would make her way to the gaming hell. The first few days she had looked for Rockwell often but he had not appeared. She could not help some disappointment at first. But why would a man like him seek her out again? He owed her nothing, not even a letter. They had said their farewell.

So she ought to turn her mind toward her customary pursuits and the constant goal of winning enough at cards to pay for the food upon their table. Her encounter with Lord Rockwell would be relegated to the past, an isolated exchange but one she would not look back upon without fondness.

"Dear, I hope it not be the creditors," her mother bemoaned.

Engrossed in her thoughts, Deana had not heard the knock at

the door. She put down her sewing.

"I shall see to it."

She opened the door to a messenger holding a brown paper package.

"For Miss Herwood," the young man said.

Looking at her name upon the package, her heartbeat quickened. She recognized the hand. After thanking the boy, she quickly stole upstairs. In the privacy of her room, she carefully untied the string. She peeled back the wrapping and, lying in the middle of red and orange silks was a familiar ivory elephant with ruby eyes. Heart pounding, she picked it up gently. Beneath the elephant lay a simple note.

For a most pleasurable evening.

Smiling, she returned the elephant tenderly to the silk. A pleasurable evening indeed. Losing a hand at cards had never proved more delightful.

THE END

Continue Deana's journey in

SUBMITTING TO HIS LORDSHIP

Submitting
TO THE
RAKE

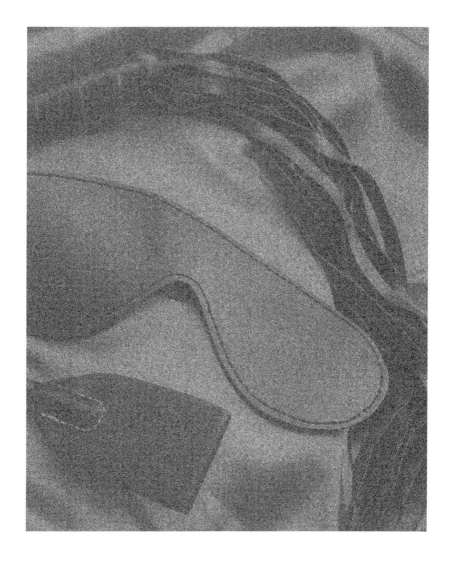

Chapter One

THOUGH THE CLOUDS SHROUDED THE night in blackness, obscuring all but shadows from view, the lone woman standing at the gates pulled her veil more securely about her face with restless, trembling hands. Every little noise—the stirring of the leaves in the trees, the scurry of some small animal, the crunch of pebbles at her feet—made her jump. At any moment she expected her cousin to descend upon her with eyes ablaze, denouncing her treachery and forswearing the sisterhood they had shared these past years.

Heloise Merrill cringed and glanced down the path, both dreading and desperate for the arrival of the carriage. Her cousin Josephine would not understand that, were it not for the affection the two of them shared, Heloise would not be standing on an open road by herself in the middle of the night, pretending to be her cousin.

She tugged at her veil.

Would the footmen recognize that she was not Josephine Merrill? Her form alone could betray her. Josephine possessed a slender body with delicate, sloping shoulders whereas Heloise had square shoulders and flesh to spare about her arms and waist. The veil hid her countenance—her round face, full cheeks and rosebud mouth. Josephine had a physiognomy that tapered at the chin, wide lips, a pert nose and slender arched brows.

The glow of a lantern approached. Heloise willed her feet to stay and not carry her back to the safety of the home she shared with her cousin and uncle, Jonathan Merrill, who had kindly taken Heloise in years ago when her parents had both succumbed to consumption. Alas, her uncle would not be home for a sennight, leaving Heloise the elder of the household. She had been tempted to send for him immediately when she had discovered the note intended for Josephine—an invitation to three shameless nights of profligacy with Sebastian Cadwell, the Earl of Blythe—but even then her uncle would not have been able to return in time. Josephine might never forgive her, but she could not allow her cousin to throw away a life of promise on a youthful fancy for a dangerous man—one of the worst rakes in England.

"Miss Merrill?" the driver inquired after alighting from his perch.

After forcing herself to exhale, Heloise nodded. Accepting his assistance with averted eyes, as if the driver might see through her veil, she stepped into the carriage. A whip cracked the air, and the carriage lurched forward. It would be hours before she arrived at her destination, the Château Follet, so named for its owner, a French expatriate.

Some dubbed it the Château of Debauchery.

How many victims had the earl claimed? Heloise wondered, unable to settle herself comfortably in the rich upholstery of the carriage seats. Neither the driver nor the footman had sneered at her or indicated in any way that they thought her a wanton woman. They did not even ask why she traveled sans a portmanteau or valise. Was it because they were accustomed to picking up women in the middle of the night for their master? Heloise shuddered to think how closely Josephine had come to ruining herself—and that prospect remained lest Heloise returned successful. She simply had to succeed. Her attempts to reason with Josephine had failed.

"What has the Earl of Blythe to recommend himself but a rugged countenance?" Heloise had asked.

"You would not understand, Heloise," Josephine had returned.

"What would I not understand?" she had pressed.

Tossing her luxuriant flaxen curls, Josephine had replied, "The ways of a man and a woman."

"I am six years your senior. You are but a babe at nine and ten. I have glimpsed more of human nature than you, Josephine."

"My dear Heloise, you may have more years than I, and I mean no cruelty, but your experience with men is decidedly limited."

Heloise had not revealed to Josephine that her experience with the opposite sex was not as lacking as Josephine would believe. Granted, Josephine had no shortage of suitors whereas Heloise had entertained but one in recent years. But the dearth of suitors had not diminished her ability to observe humankind, and she knew a rogue when she saw one. People had a tendency to overlook the shortcomings in a man such as Sebastian Cadwell because of his title, wealth and breeding.

When it had become clear that her disapproval of Josephine's choice of company was having the unintended consequence of making her cousin even more attached to Sebastian, Heloise had attempted to reason with the earl himself. She had requested an audience with him on numerous occasions, but he had refused all of her attempts to engage him in conversation until she had managed one evening to accost him as he emerged from his box at the theater.

"I WOULD HAVE A WORD WITH you, your lordship," Heloise had said hastily before he could turn to ignore her.

He had stared down at her with brown eyes so dark they appeared black. With dark hair waving over a wide brow, the firm, square jaw of a man who knows what he wants and a subtle cleft of the chin to denote a masculinity matured, the earl was more imposing than she remembered. His stylish hat sat at smart attention upon his head. His double-breasted coat with matching high collar fit him snugly, emphasizing his broad shoulders and tall frame. Lord Blythe had always been considered a swell of the first stare.

"You have not responded to my written requests to speak with you," she added, trying not to be intimidated by his height. He seemed to command more space than his body actually occupied. "I think it rather discourteous of you not to have granted me an audience."

He smiled—an unnerving curl of the lips. Sensuous lips. Heloise snapped her attention to the matter at hand. Gracious, why was she staring at the man's lips?

"You would find me more discourteous, I assure you, had I accepted your request, Miss Merrill."

At her surprised pause, he continued, "I know what it is you intend to speak to me of, and I had thought to spare us both from the conclusion you would draw of me upon hearing my response."

His words took her breath away.

"Ah, I was right," he noted. "I can tell at this moment you think me audacious and arrogant."

She flushed, perturbed that he should have correctly guessed her thoughts.

"Let us now part ways," he suggested, "before I offend you further."

Heloise attempted to grab at words, to form some manner of coherent retort, but failed. Worse still, she had not realized her mouth hung open until he curled his forefinger gently beneath her chin and closed her lips. Horrified, she was only too glad when he tipped his hat and took his leave. Her heart was pounding madly—she wished from anger alone but had to admit it was his touch that had unsettled her more. A warm wave had rushed over her body, and she understood for the first time how Josephine could be captivated by this man. A man she had hitherto disdained. And now considered more dangerous than ever.

THERE WOULD BE NO MOUTH dumbly agape this time, Heloise promised herself as the Château Follet loomed before her. She intended to provide Sebastian Cadwell the set-down he deserved. This time she was prepared to do battle and emerge the victor. If she did not, she would have risked her cousin's affection for naught. For hours after discovering the letter from the earl, Heloise had struggled with the idea of reasoning with Josephine again. Surely Josephine knew that the earl would merely use her for the pleasures of the flesh, then cast her aside as he had done with so many women before her? But the numerous suitors that Josephine had entertained must have engendered many a romantic notion in her young head.

Or worse, perhaps Josephine would not care.

This was the only way, Heloise affirmed to herself as she alighted from the carriage. Waiting at the steps of the château, an abigail named Annabelle greeted her quietly and gently.

"I will show you to your room, madam," Annabelle said.

Heloise considered scurrying back into the carriage. Perhaps there was another means to accomplish her goal, one that she had overlooked, one that did not require her to be here? But when she turned to seek the carriage, it had disappeared around the corner.

What a ninny you are, Heloise Merrill, she chided herself. She had heard scandalous things occurred at the home of Madame Follet, a French widow rumored to have known the notorious Marquis de Sade in her previous life.

The abigail showed Heloise upstairs to a room that was surely inspired by Sade's *The 120 Days of Sodom*. On the walls, accompanying the gilded candelabras, hung whips, chains, lashes, collars, shackles and other paraphernalia she could not place. Besides the customary furniture—a magnificent bed with cornices atop its posts and a pleated valance, a veneered writing desk, a sofa and chairs upholstered in silk, a mahogany chest of drawers and a vanity with inlaid top—the chamber housed a mysterious post, a wooden bench, an apparatus that reminded her of a medieval rack, and sets of ropes dangling from the ceiling. Despite the ominous accoutrements, the many golden candelabras and the floral silk wallpaper adorning the walls lent a comforting warmth to the room.

"His Lordship requested this room for you," Annabelle explained. "It be our finest. We call it the Empress Room."

"Is…is His Lordship here?" Heloise inquired, trying not to stare about.

"He arrives soon, I believe, but he has arranged for your wardrobe. Shall I assist you now into your nightdress?"

"That won't be necessary," Heloise responded, stepping away before the woman could touch her.

Annabelle look puzzled.

"I shall ring if I find I need your assistance, shall I?"

Annabelle frowned, perhaps wondering if Heloise would summon her from her bed at an inconvenient time.

"You are welcome to retire for the evening," Heloise assured her. She had no intention of staying for long. Once she was done with the earl, she would request a post-chaise to take her home. Taking a seat on the bed, she waited for Sebastian Cadwell.

SEBASTIAN HANDED HIS HAT AND gloves to one of Madame Follet's footmen and considered heading up to the room where Josephine Merrill would be waiting. He paused, lacking desire. Indeed, he had had little inclination to invite her here, but the minx had worn down his resistance. Her determination had pleased his vanity. It had been years since he had allowed himself to be embroiled in a relationship with one as young as Miss Josephine, but her youthfulness belied her familiarity with men. He knew she had lifted her skirts beneath at least two friends of his.

Not looking in upon her would be impolite. Perhaps she would still be asleep. Would he attempt to wake her with a kiss or would he be relieved and head to his own room for a moment of solitude?

What the bloody hell is the matter with me? He had never hesitated before, had never known his eros to waver. He enjoyed all manner of women. Why not the lovely and charming Josephine Merrill? His friends, if they knew his thoughts, would question his manhood or suggest that old age was settling in upon him though he had turned but two and thirty earlier this year.

"Cadwell, *mon cheri!*" Marguerite Follet greeted him. The lady of the house, in stylish *dishabille* and a golden turban, looked radiant, as much a beauty at forty as she had been at twenty.

Sebastian kissed her extended hand.

"My maid tells me your lady friend arrived," she notified him. "She is not what I would have ascribed to your tastes. She seems almost *virginal.* I thought you never did virgins."

"I don't," he responded resolutely.

"Ah, then there is more than meets the eye with your mademoiselle. I think, at the least, you need have no worry from Lord Devon."

Sebastian thought her comment strange, for Lord Devon had been known to try his luck with all the maidens at Lady Follet's.

"I warn you he arrived yesterday and has with him *two* ladybirds. *Twin sisters,*" Lady Follet continued. "And Anne Wesley is here as well. I do wish Lord Harsdale would stop inviting her. I dread unhappy people, and she is as acrimonious as they come. You would not believe what she said to me—that you were a lover of *middling* abilities."

He started. That had never been said of him before.

"Of course she speaks from a bitter heart. Everyone knows how long she pined for you."

Had Anne counterfeited the ecstatic cries—cries so loud he had thought he might never hear properly again—when she had been with him? Sebastian wondered. It was hard to believe. He had never questioned his intuition when it came to the art of lovemaking. Nonetheless, he felt a stir in his groin.

"Goodness knows there are few to equal you where *that* is concerned," Lady Follet added with a telling flush in her cheeks. "When you are done with your mademoiselle and have a wish to renew your acquaintance with *me*…"

Sebastian bowed, recalling with fondness the moments of passion they had shared on occasion. "You honor me, my lady."

A sigh escaped her lips. "I would that it be soon, Cadwell. I fear one day you will have no use for me and my château."

"That could never be."

Her golden-brown eyes surveyed him with a depth he had never felt before. "I wonder, Cadwell, that you might not some-day take a mistress or more permanent lover? Even a wife?"

"My record speaks for itself. Any woman who accepts my invitation understands that the three nights here represent the end, not the beginning, of an affair."

"And have you never requested to see a woman again when you have done with her here?"

"Never. What better way to conclude a liaison than with three nights of unforgettable passion? Why wait until I tire of her or she of me? Why tempt what would no doubt be an awkward or painful end?"

"What a pragmatist you are, Cadwell."

He inclined his head in acknowledgement.

"Love knows no pragmatism."

"My dear," Sebastian said, eying her with care, "have you partaken of tainted waters?"

Lady Follet pursed her lips. "It is only…well, your lady…never mind. I will not keep you."

With a gracious bow and kiss to her hand, he took his leave and headed up the stairs to see Miss Josephine. He resolved that he would make it worth her while. He certainly would not have her echoing Anne Wesley's sentiments, fabricated or otherwise. The halls would ring with the cries of joy he would wrest from his lovely guest. And then he would bid Miss Josephine *adieu*, as he had to the dozens of others who had preceded her, and send he on her way to a better future.

As he headed down the hall, he felt a renewed sense of spirit. The desire he had lacked moments ago returned with new vigor. He would take Miss Josephine, awake or not, into his arms and have her swooning like never before.

HELOISE CLASPED AND UNCLASPED HER hands several times as she stood looking out the window at the descending moon. To her surprise, she had fallen asleep for an hour or two on the luxurious feather mattress. She was hungry and considering ringing the maid for something to eat when she heard footsteps approaching. It was *him*. Somehow she knew it was him. The long strides, the swift and confident tread could belong to none other than the Earl of Blythe.

A knock, and then the door opened. Heloise continued to stare out the window, telling herself that she would not be intimidated by this man.

"Good evening, my dear…"

Letting out a breath, Heloise turned to face him. He stood on the threshold, his form filling much of the doorframe. His tailored cutaway coat with brass buttons, fitted buff pantaloons, perfectly tied cravat and gleaming Hessians made her aware of how mussed her own appearance must be, her gown rumpled from having fallen asleep on the bed and her hair flying in wisps about her face. His eyes narrowed at her. Feeling herself falter beneath his imposing gaze, she lifted her chin.

"Where is Miss Josephine?" he asked.

The coldness in his tone sent a shiver down her spine. Bracing herself, she replied, "Safe from harm. Safe from you."

"Harm? What harm did you imagine she would come to?"

That he should ask that question amazed and riled her. Did he think her a simpleton?

"Surely you could not be so dull of wit, Your lordship?" she returned, pleased that she managed a rejoinder. "You may be devoid of morals but I thought at least you did not lack in perception."

Little flames lit his eyes.

"You would take her innocence and ruin her," Heloise accused.

"Innocence?" he echoed. "Miss Merrill, how well do you know your cousin?"

She took a sharp breath. The man was insufferable.

"Better than you," Heloise said. "She is far too respectable a person to merit your attentions."

Is that a smirk floating on his lips? she wondered.

"She is indeed," he allowed, "and as such will not suffer the injury you fear."

"It is quite well known what manner of depravity occurs here, sir!"

"No one save Lady Follet would have known she was here— lest you spoke of it."

Heloise felt her cheeks burning at the suggestion that she would have exposed her cousin.

"I spoke of this to no one when I intercepted your note to her," she said. "And how could you protect her identity here? You will forgive me if I do not profess great confidence in the likes of Lady Follet!"

"Miss Merrill, you are free to believe what you will. As for Lady Follet, you speak too hastily of a lady you know not," he said with an edge to his voice.

Heloise felt a stab of remorse for speaking harshly, but she had no need for the likes of *him* to point that out to her.

"I assumed..." she attempted, noticing with worry that the pupils of his eyes constricted.

"Why are you here, Miss Merrill?"

"You would not grant me an audience. And I would have you listen to me. I would have you listen!"

The earl folded his arms and waited. His frown did not diminish.

"If there is a shred of decency in you," she began.

He lifted his brows. "I thought I was devoid of morals."

She winced, regretting her earlier words, but there was nothing to be done. She could not retract what she had said, so she forged ahead.

"You have no need of someone like Josephine. Someone of your, well, stature can command any number of other women. Josephine is not worth your time."

"Rather harsh words for a cousin you adore."

"I meant—" she bristled.

"I know what you meant, Miss Merrill, but my mind has not changed on the matter since last we met, and I do not appreciate attempts to meddle in my affairs. I wonder that your cousin approves of it, but I take it she does not realize you are here?"

Again, she flushed. "I am here on her behalf, even if she would not approve of what I do. I realize I risk her affection, but I could not stand idly by and watch her demise. She may not know it, but she requires my aid."

"Noble if not condescending sentiments. Your cousin is a grown woman, not in leading strings."

"She is young and does not appreciate the arts a man of your sort would employ."

This time it was he who turned color. "A man of my sort?"

Would he have her explain all to him? Heloise wondered, sensing a dangerous pit opening up before her.

"I think you know to what I allude," she evaded.

"If by that you mean your shallow view of my association with women…"

Heloise blinked. *He* was the rake and would yet criticize *her* character? The man was beyond monstrous.

He continued, "I quite understand people of *your* sort and how threatened you feel by my enlightened position on the fairer sex."

"Enlightened? Is that how you defend your wanton ways?"

He clucked his tongue. "Tsk, tsk. You make it sound vulgar, Miss Merrill. Why scorn the innate urges, the natural passions of our bodies?"

Her heart began to pound once more. Something in the way he spoke, the rich tenor of his voice, the enunciation—as if he were caressing the words—made her skin warm.

"The rhetoric of one who lacks the resolve to resist the base desires…" she began, but her tone lacked confidence even to her own ears.

He took a step toward her, and despite the lethargy she had felt from her journey and lack of sleep, every nerve in her body came to life.

"Are you possessed of such resolve, Miss Merrill?" he inquired.

His gaze seemed to probe into her past, and she was sure he saw it all.

"That is none of your concern and irrelevant to the matter at hand," she said quickly.

"You made it my concern when you chose to meddle in my affairs," he replied grimly, advancing another step.

"I think I am not possessed of the same, er, passions as you," she answered, taking a step back.

"Indeed? How sad. Perhaps that can be changed."

"I have no wish to change."

"You may feel differently in three days' time."

Three days' time? What did he mean by that? Instinctively, she glanced toward the door, her escape, but it was too far. And *he* stood in her path.

"I have no plans to keep my own company for the next three days," he elaborated. "And as you have deprived me of Miss Josephine, you will have to take her place."

"I have no intention of staying," she protested, trying to stave off the panic that gripped her heart. But it was not the fear of immediate harm that alarmed her. It was…the flush of excitement coursing in her body, a sensation reminiscent of a time long ago when she did not ignore her curiosity or the urges of the flesh.

"Your intentions matter not. My coach will return you home only on my command."

"You mean to keep me here? Against my will?" she cried.

"You came of your own free will, Miss Merrill. I would have advised against it."

"I am to be your prisoner?" She attempted with what little indignation she could muster to mask her agitation.

He advanced toward her, but she stepped back until the back of her knees struck the bed. The nearness of his body took the air from her. The flush in her body grew.

"Do you know what I do with meddlers?" he asked.

Trapped between him and the bed behind her, all she could do was hold his gaze. Her mind grasped for a rejoinder but came up empty.

"I punish them, Miss Merrill."

Chapter Two

HE SAW FEAR IN THOSE bright almond-shaped eyes of hers. *Good*, Sebastian thought. The little meddler needed a lesson.

Blocked from escape, she reminded him of a mouse trapped in a corner. He advanced a final step toward her, taking away the last shred of space between them, daring her to speak. Her silence gratified him. He waited to see if she would push him away or slap him in the face—he had received his fair share of those from women desperate to hold on to a semblance of propriety when inwardly they yearned to be seduced—but such an action would require her to touch him, and Miss Merrill leaned away from him so that her bosom would not graze his chest.

"You…" She faltered.

With one motion, he grasped her by the wrist, brought her arm behind her, and pushed her over his knees as he sat upon the bed.

Miss Merrill inhaled sharply but did not struggle. She lay still on top of him.

Sebastian observed the curve of her rump through her muslin and felt a sudden tug at his crotch. His hand itched to palm her arse, but he had meant only to scare her, not punish her.

"We could start with a good spanking," he said.

Was that a whimper he heard? As she was lying facedown, he could not see her expression. She made no movement. Curious, he placed his hand on the arch of one buttock. This time she flinched but remained where she was, even though he had loosened his hold on her wrist enough that she could have wrested herself away from him.

She wants to be spanked, he realized. A low, burning desire pulsed in his cock. Despite his earlier suggestion that she take the place of her cousin, he was all too cognizant that Miss Heloise Merrill was not Miss Josephine. Nonetheless, he was not a man to deprive a woman.

Raising his hand above her, he brought it down on the buttock he had caressed seconds before—sharp enough to command attention but tame compared to what he was accustomed to delivering. Again she flinched but said nothing. There was more to this Miss Merrill than he had first perceived. To his further surprise, he felt a maddening rush of desire crashing into him. Desire he had lacked earlier. He suddenly wanted to show Miss Merrill all the joys of Château Follet. Wanted to take her senses to a realm she had never known before.

He tempered his desire. This was Heloise Merrill. Not some bit of muslin. He slapped her other cheek through her gown. Her arse had such a lovely, substantive curve to it. Some women appeared to have no arse at all. He wanted to see Miss Merrill bare. Wanted to feel her plumpness. He decided he would and massaged one buttock. *Superb.* He would enjoy giving her a sound spanking.

No. He intended to give her a set-down—not to engage in anything more.

As if coming to her senses, Miss Merrill tried to push herself up. He promptly pushed her back down. Now came her indignation, the blush of anger, but she would see that she was no match for him.

"I'm not finished with you yet," he told her. "Lie still."

She either did not perceive or chose not to listen to his directive for she continued to struggle. The grinding of her pelvis against his thigh caused the blood to course boldly through his groin.

"Lie still," he commanded again and emphasized his words with a harsher slap to her derrière. God, how he wanted to hear the

sound of her arse sans the gown and petticoats, but he had to
proceed with patience with this one. He wanted to frighten her
a little—that was part of the arousal—but he also wanted her to
trust him.

"I am loath to issue my demands twice, Miss Merrill," he
informed her. "Now take your punishment like a good girl."

He could guess her internal dialogue. She *was* a good girl. That
was perhaps the problem. Perhaps she had never been punished
and was bored with being the good girl. Perhaps she had been
punished too often before she became the good girl and wanted
a return to the days when she wasn't so good.

She lay still across his thigh as he delivered several sharp blows.
Was it his imagination or had she lifted her arse higher to greet
his hand? He smacked her several more times before pausing to
note her quickened breath, the stillness of her body and the flush
upon her skin. His own body felt warm and he wished he had
removed his coat earlier. His cock was hard with the weight of
her upon him.

"How did that please you, Miss Merrill?" he asked, his breath
less steady than he would have liked.

"Please me?" she returned, incredulous.

"But of course. Why do you think women come here willingly
if it were not pleasurable?"

She had no answer, so he continued. "That is the beauty of the
debauchery you were so hasty to condemn. The irony of what
occurs here at Château Follet is that the more you dread it, fear it,
disdain it, the more you enjoy it."

"Impossible," she murmured.

"Is it?"

He reached toward her ankle and slid his hand under the hem
of her gown. She gasped when his hand came in contact with her
stocking-clad leg. Her body jumped at the touch, but she could
do far worse if she truly loathed what was happening. Gently he
drifted his hand up the silk until he reached the softness of her
bare thigh—a hundred times smoother and more delectable than
the feel of silk. Heady with anticipation, he reached under her

arse, between her thighs, and when he connected with her wet-ness, he closed his eyes, his breath ragged.

The blood was pounding in his cock, and he allowed a husky quality to creep into his voice. "Your body, Miss Merrill, proves the possibilities."

Running his hand around her thigh, he palmed a buttock. *Glorious.* He grasped the flesh more firmly and heard her groan. Flipping the dress and petticoats over her waist, he laid bare the prize. Two perfectly rounded orbs, as unblemished as those of a babe, gleamed in the dim light of the candles. He licked his bottom lip as if he were about to feed on a succulent cut of beefsteak. He delivered a sharp slap with the back of his hand and watched in delight as the mound of flesh quivered.

"How many, Miss Merrill?"

"Hmmm?" came the dazed voice from beneath the layers of fabric.

He gave her a formidable swat.

"Four," she answered quickly.

Sebastian smiled to himself. She could be trained.

"Eight it is," he said. "If I have to repeat myself again, we will triple the number."

Greedily, his hand slapped at her arse. The smack of bare flesh to bare flesh rang in his ears as melodious as a symphony. When he was done, he gazed with satisfaction at the red imprints his hand had left upon her pale skin. He could smell her arousal and confirmed it when he slid his hand between her and found her wetter than before. His erection pressed painfully against her hip.

Abruptly, he stood and dragged her to the post.

"What are you—" she protested when he pulled her wrists around the post and tied them overhead with silken rope.

The hemp he would save for another time.

Another time? Sebastian silently cursed himself. What the bloody hell was the matter with him?

Stepping back, he admired her form pressed against the post, which cleaved her breasts and separated the globes to either side. Miss Merrill was not unattractive. Her rounded figure reminded him of Ruben's portrait of Hélène Fourment. Supple. Ripe. He could see himself entwining his fingers in her lustrous dark hair. She had a complexion free of blemish and that required little in the way of powder or rouge. And those voluptuous lips…

A sense of remorse crept into him as he observed how Miss Merrill's bottom lips quivered. She had very full lips. More succulent than her cousin's. He wondered how such lips would feel beneath his own. He imagined taking her mouth would be like sinking into a rich, sweet strawberry.

His head swam with lust, and he needed to clear it before he did something he did not intend—such as tearing the clothes from her and ravishing her. He reminded himself of the anger that he had felt earlier. The impudence of this woman, to foil his plans for a pleasant weekend and deprive him of the joys of exploring Miss Josephine's lovely body. The effrontery of her to stand there in judgment of him with those wide brown eyes—eyes possessed of such clarity that he could see every emotion through them. He almost feared looking into them too deeply.

Worst of all, she had had the audacity to speak to his own reservations where Miss Josephine was concerned.

"Miss Merrill, I leave you to contemplate your situation."

Her eyes widened and pleaded with him.

He could not let her go—did not want to let her go—but could not trust himself to stay. His cock, hard as the post she was tied to, stretched agonizingly. He turned, avoiding her gaze for fear that he could too easily give in to those doe-like eyes, and left her to seek the reprieve of his own chambers and ponder what the hell he was to do with her next.

HELOISE YANKED AT HER BINDINGS with enough desperation to cause the rope to chafe against her wrists. She simply had to escape.

But escape from what? a sardonic voice inside her asked. From his exquisite touch? From facing the fact that she had, indeed, enjoyed what he had done to her—that her body had been aroused to wetness by it?

She shook her head vehemently at the voice. Who knew what other devious plans the earl had in store for her? The spanking had been relatively harmless—though her arse still smarted from it—but she only had to look at the frightful instruments hanging on the wall to know that a world of darker possibilities lay within Lord Blythe. She eyed the riding crop. *"The more you dread it, fear it, disdain it, the more you enjoy it."* Those had been his words. She contemplated the pain the riding crop could induce. Could she derive pleasure from such pain?

Warmth flared in her loins. Why did the mere thought titillate her? Her curiosity surprised her, but it was curiosity that killed the cat. Perhaps it was curiosity that had compelled her cousin to want to be here, but she would not fall victim to the same.

She strained once again at her bonds, her arms sore from their position, and attempted to undo the knot, chipping three of her fingernails in the process. *There simply has to be a way out.*

The door opened and the earl appeared, a touch disheveled but no less dapper. He had removed his coat and loosened his cravat. She stared at the sinews of his throat and felt a wave of warmth washing over her. She quelled it.

"Miss Merrill, I have decided—" he began.

"You will set me free or pay dearly for it," she informed him hotly.

He paused, then raised his brows in amusement—a reaction that only fueled her anger.

"My uncle will see you brought before a magistrate," she continued. "If you do not release me, then prepare to spend your time at Newgate."

He crossed his arms and leaned against the wall. His bemusement when he should have been daunted by her threats both infuriated and worried her.

"On what charges would I be sent to Newgate?" he asked.

Damn his insolence, Heloise fumed.

"On kidnapping!" she snapped. "And...and surely there are laws against this..."

"This what, Miss Merrill?"

"You know quite well to what I allude!"

She pulled at her bonds for emphasis, but he continued to wait for her elucidation. She let out a sigh of exasperation.

"Of forcing your attentions upon me!"

To her horror, he laughed. He pulled away from the wall. "Tell me, Miss Merrill, did you not come here of your own free will?"

She bristled. "Yes, but—"

"My coachman was not under orders to abduct anyone."

"Yes, but—"

He took a step toward her. "Did you not lie willingly across my lap?"

Her flush of consternation began to pale.

"You—"

"And requested I spank you four times?"

"I did n—"

"And *enjoyed* it?"

He stood a breath away from her, invading her space and further scattering her thoughts. Her volleys had not struck their target. She needed a new approach.

"How would you explain to a magistrate that you submitted against your will when the evidence reveals your pleasure?"

"Please," Heloise attempted. "Surely you are not without conscience or sensibility…"

"Only devoid of morals," he reminded her.

She swallowed at the verbal blow but pressed on. "You can understand why I might—why I thought I had no other recourse?"

After probing the depths of her gaze he stepped away from her. Without the intrusion of his body, she took an easier breath.

"It is no small effort you have made to protect your cousin's virtue," he acknowledged. "Indeed, you have risked your own ruin to save her."

"I will explain to my family that a dear friend took ill and I went to visit her."

"In the middle of the night? Without packing a valise?"

"I was beside myself."

"I find it hard to believe that Miss Merrill could ever be so discomposed."

"My uncle will have no reason to doubt my word."

"And what of Josephine? What will you tell her?"

"I will beg her forgiveness and hope that she will, in time, come to understand the wisdom of my action."

"Perhaps that will come to pass," he said as he began to walk around her. "Or more likely, she will find another man to whom she can attach her fancy and forget her lost invitation to the Château."

Heloise found herself having to agree with the earl. Nonetheless, she professed, "I hope someone who merits her affection. Someone who will make her happy."

"And what do you hope for yourself, Miss Merrill?"

The question was an unexpected strike. No one had ever asked her that before.

"Myself?"

"What sort of man will you marry or take a fancy to?"

"This is hardly a subject—"

"Pray tell you do not see yourself as a lonely spinster, content after some time to marry a kindly but boring vicar with limited prospects."

That he could guess the precise future she had foreseen for herself disgruntled her.

"That would be better than succumbing to a rake," she retorted.

To her further disconcertion, he laughed. "Do you know what I think, Miss Merrill?"

"I do not *care* what you think, Lord Blythe."

He was standing behind her now—which was worse than when he stood in front of her for now she could not see him. She could only feel his heat.

He leaned toward her. "I think you wanted to come here for yourself. I think if you had been in Josephine's place, you would have accepted my invitation and been furious at anyone who tried to stop you."

Her gaze blurred. She trembled inside. *Good heavens, could it be true?*

STEPPING TOWARD HER, SEBASTIAN LIGHTLY grazed the curve of her rump. It proved a mistake. He could breathe in her scent—not the scent of her soap or perfume, but something deeper, something that could best be described as her essence—and it made the blood in him pound. His cock reared its head. He would have ripped the clothes from her and fucked her there against the post if he had lacked the resolve she had so flippantly questioned earlier.

Hell and damnation. After having convinced himself in his room earlier that he had provided Miss Merrill a decent set-down, he had returned, prepared to set her free and see her off home. But then she had hurled those threats of hers. And looked so damn delicious tied to the post, still flush with arousal.

For the first time, he had no plan, knew not what he intended. He knew only that his hands itched to touch her, grab her, make her quiver with pleasure.

"Submit to me."

He knew not from whence the words had come, but suddenly his clothes were too warm. He undid his neckcloth completely.

Silence from her. He considered pressing his erection against her derrière, but he needed her reply. There had been women from whom he sought no consent for he knew full well their desire to be taken. And so he had played the game with them, he the ravisher and they the willing victims.

But not with Miss Merrill. A light spanking was one matter. For what he truly wished to do to her, he wanted her acquiescence. Her submission. Her surrender.

"Submit to me," he repeated, softly. "You can trust me."

Though he could not see the expression upon her face, he could sense her defenses coming down. He needed them to come down faster.

"You have such lovely hips, Heloise."

She perked up at the sound of her name and allowed him to place his hands upon her. He grasped her hips, the flare of which her gown could not hide. What wonderful handles they would provide if he chose to fuck her hard from behind.

"And the most delightful arse."

She was likely blushing at the compliment.

He caressed a buttock, then placed his mouth near her ear. "There is so much that can be done here...and here."

He trailed his hand up one side of her arm to her wrist and down the other before cupping a breast. "And here."

A pause. "Such as?"

Ah, he had stimulated her curiosity. Good.

"Anything you wish."

With both hands he manhandled her breasts, eliciting a low groan from her.

"These," he said, "can be fondled, kissed, bitten, pinched, slapped—by hand or by any of the instruments you see before you. We could fasten clamps to your nipples, pinch the flesh with pins, tie them until they turn red with anger, adorn them with molten wax..."

Her bosom heaved against his hands.

"Have you had such attentions upon your breasts before, Miss Merrill?"

"No," she murmured.

"Has a man ever taken pleasure from your body?"

He half expected her to rebuke him that such matters were none of his affair, but she replied, "Two. There were two."

Two too many, he thought while impressed, not by the revelation, but by her honesty. Given her obdurate protection of her cousin's virtue, one might expect to find Miss Merrill beyond reproach in regards to her own, but Sebastian knew human fallibility all too well and was relieved to find she was no virgin. That he was not her only encounter roused an unexpected jealousy in his chest. Such a feeling was not common for he had, in the past, often shared his women with the other patrons at Château Follet.

"And did they pleasure you?"

"It was many years ago. We were young."

Just as well she did not answer him directly, Sebastian decided.

He was confident he could surpass any experience she might have had and had no desire to know the particulars.

"Then you understand the yearnings of the flesh," he said, sliding his hands down her ribs back to her hips. His fingers slowly gathered her skirts upward. The blood pounded in his head as the image of their naked bodies rutting against the post flashed in his eye. "I may be devoid of morals, but I am no hypocrite."

She stiffened, but he dared hazard her indignation would be short-lived. His fingers continued to lift her skirts.

"Tell me, Miss Merrill, why you find it so depraved to indulge our prurient desires?"

"I don't," she protested. "My censure lies in your seduction of innocent young women."

He did not bother correcting her that it was Josephine who had seduced him, but instead replied, "I willingly engage and seek the companionship of women with similar appetites."

That gave her pause. Apparently it had not occurred to her that he was not the only one guilty of lust. His fingers grazed her thigh as he continued, "I think it immoral of you to impose your sense of morality on others and to deny women the pleasures of the flesh."

"*I* am immoral?" she responded in disbelief. "Because I am not a libertine?"

"Because you would bar fulfillment from others for no purpose."

He slipped his hand between her thighs.

"No purpose, my lord? Protecting a loved one from shame, from risking her future is not reason enough for you?"

He found her clitoris and began a gentle caress. "In whose eyes would she be shamed?"

"Need—need you ask? In the eyes of...polite society."

Her breaths became shallow as he stroked the sensitive nub.

"Setting aside the premise that there is a single pervading norm—which I would dispute—are the darlings of the *beau monde* always right?"

"It matters not if society is right or wrong."

"How convenient," he said ironically, deepening his touch. "What if it were wrong? Ours is a society that once burned people they thought were witches, sanctioned the trading of fellow humans as slaves, governed without representation of the people. By abiding by its norms and following its standards, are you not guilty of supporting its immorality?"

He sensed her thoughts swirling, the wheels of her mind turning, and felt a strange thrill, more exciting than any seduction he had undertaken before. Slipping a finger toward her quim, he discovered her wet with desire. Arousal raged in his cock. He was almost there.

"You would believe," she said, still trying to persevere with her own judgment, "that not allowing a woman to become wanton is somehow immoral?"

"Precisely. The suppression of freedom is rarely a good thing. Make no mistake, I do not encourage recklessness or condone any impulse that is criminal. But why should we condemn what are but natural urges of every man and every woman?"

She was gasping as his fingers plied their trade, striking her sensitive spot over and over.

"It may be natural for *you*, my lord."

He fitted his body against hers. Marvelous. The contrast of her soft body against his hardness. With his length, he pushed her into the pole.

"Do you suggest you have no such urges, Miss Merrill?"

He ground his desire into her. Her arms tightened against the pole.

"I do not let such urges overwhelm me."

She clearly knew not what she said for her body indicated otherwise.

"Why not?"

No answer. But her thighs parted for his fingers to conduct their ministrations. He plunged a finger into her quim. She instantly clenched about his digit. He plunged another finger into her as he continued to circle her clitoris with his thumb. She trembled between him and the pole, gasping and groaning, groaning and gasping. Her climax loomed near.

"I think, Heloise," he said in a low, husky tone next to her ear, "you should surrender to your natural urges. Allow yourself to indulge in the sublime and submit to me."

Though her body was clearly responding to him, he still wanted to hear her say it. There would be no triumph until she did. When she did not reply, he withdrew his hand. She let out an anguished cry.

"Submit to me," he tried again.

Her hips ground against him, in search of his hand. He teased her lightly with his fingers, but not enough to make her spend. She moaned.

"Submit."

Her voice was shaky but the sentence clear.

"Yes…yes, I submit."

⟨≈❀≈⟩

AN INFERNO OF YEARNING ENGULFED her body. Desperate for his touch, for release, Heloise had agreed to submit to the Earl of Blythe. The delectable beginning—of feeling his body pressing hers into the post, of his skilled fingers teasing her body to arousal—had become a divine torture. She felt as if she would go mad if she did not spend, and yet, she exalted in the precipice from which her body dangled. She understood that she *wanted* to submit to him.

And she was not the only one whose desire had been sparked. His erection, hard as stone, pressed against the arch of her arse. That awareness made her cunny ache, made what he did to her all the more pleasing. Her legs threatened to buckle and her arms begged for liberation from their bonds, but she would not give in until she had attained her climax.

She waited for him to resume his stroking. She heard him take a ragged breath. Then felt him step away from her.

What the bloody…

She had agreed to submit to him! Surely he would reward her now. Her nerves trembled like the vibrations of a tuning fork, seeking the proper conclusion.

Damnation, she cursed to herself when still he did nothing. What a fool she was to think that she could expect better from a rake! Had she not accused him of lacking morals? Granted, she knew her statement to have been in the extreme—she suspected he *did* have a conscience or she would have thought all attempts to reason with him hopeless—but he was proving her words now. Well, if he would not help her, she would satisfy herself. She tilted her hips and attempted to grind her mons against the post.

"Stop it," he ordered.

When she refused to obey, he found her nipple and squeezed it—hard. She yelped and stopped.

"You have much to learn, Miss Merrill."

He was back to addressing her formally. She had liked it when he called her 'Heloise'. On his tongue, the name, which she had hitherto found plain, sounded beautiful, inviting and seductive.

"You're a blackguard," she said through gritted teeth.

"Resorting to insults now, are we?" he responded.

"I should have known not to expect better—"

Threading his fingers through her hair, he massaged her scalp with both hands, coaxing her resistance away and easing her into a quasi-meditative state. But then he jolted her from the tender complacency when he fisted his hands in her hair and jerked her head back.

"Have you ever stood naked before a man?" he asked into her ear.

Her heart throbbed, pressing itself against her chest walls as if it had grown too large for its compartment.

There had been an attempt with the son of the squire, but her stays had exasperated the young man. He had thrown her skirts above her waist and penetrated her before prudence, made sluggish by the carnal distress in her own body, could prevail. In the most unceremonious of minutes she had lost her virtue. But amidst the aftermath of shame and fear was a guilty satisfaction, a smugness even, of having discovered the taboo reserved only for couples lawfully joined. Having given of herself already, what was left for her to forsake? Why not indulge her desires? The experiences of her youth could not compare to this though, and a part of her yearned to revel in what might come from a man of greater…artistry.

"Have you?" he repeated.

"No," she replied.

"You are about to," he informed her, unbuttoning the back of her gown.

Her pulse quickened. It did not take long for him to push the top part of her garment off her shoulders and toward her wrists. He unpinned the skirt and untied the petticoats. They pooled at her feet. He unlaced her stays with the swiftness of the most practiced chambermaid. In little time, she found herself standing in her chemise, stockings and shoes. Little bumps lighted her skin at her state of undress. Did he mean to proceed further? Would she find herself, as he had suggested, naked before him? What if he did not like what he saw? He had expected the company of Josephine, after all.

Reaching around her, he grabbed her breasts through the chemise. Of a sudden, she yearned to feel his powerful hands upon her bare flesh. She would arch her breasts further into his hand were it not for the post pressing into her sternum. He fingered the seam of her chemise, and she realized with embarrassment that she had not selected one of her finer, less worn undergarments. Fisting the fabric in one hand, he wrenched it against her body.

"Wait!" she gasped. "I haven't—"

Too late. The chemise ripped away from her, scalding the skin where it had most resisted. She took in a sharp breath as if cold had blasted her body, but it was not the air she found chilling. She had no undergarments to wear home. And now she stood with all of her in plain view of his probing eyes—eyes that surely missed little, eyes that were examining every inch of her. What was he thinking? Why did he not speak?

Crossing over to the wall, he removed an instrument and went to stand behind her once again. Why did he not stand so that she could see him? It was unsettling not being able to read his face or know what he might do next. She rested her forehead against the post. Part of her was more aware, more alive, than she had ever been before. Part of her wanted only to disappear into the ground. This had been a mistake. She was not ready for this.

He struck the crop against the post above her head, making her jump.

"The nine-tail and single-tail are also delectable," he murmured into her ear. "Your safety word is 'Madrid'. Ever been to Spain, Miss Merrill?"

The crop. He had taken the crop. What did he intend with it?

"Miss Merrill, I asked you a question."

"No," she answered.

"It is worth a visit. If you wish to be released, speak 'Madrid' and I shall stop. Otherwise, you may cry as loud as you wish. You may protest, wail, plead, beg or sob, but only 'Madrid' will set you free."

She groaned. Ready or not, she wanted this. Her cunny pulsed with anticipation.

Whack!

The crop stung her buttock. He allowed her a moment to register the sensation before landing another. The pain was sharper, more concentrated, than the blows he had delivered by hand. He struck her three, four, five more times, his backhand as potent as his forehand. She gritted her teeth against the burn. Her entire arse felt as if it were on fire. On the twelfth whack, she cried out and tears stung her eyes.

"I will release one of your hands," he told her. "You will pleasure yourself."

Pleasure herself? In front of him? But masturbation was the most private of acts. The notion of touching her genitals before him was horrifying, lewd, sinful, wicked...provocative.

He coaxed her into action with a strike that made her wonder how she would ever be able to sit again. Her hand flew to her mons and she rubbed two fingers against her clitoris. It was awkward with the post in the way. She had to arch her derrière to provide her hand enough access. At first she felt only shame. There was nothing pleasurable about fondling herself before Lord

Blythe. He had sauntered to the side for a better view. But when she chanced to meet his smoldering gaze, saw the slight ripple of muscle above his jaw, desire flamed in her loins. She rubbed herself more purposefully, making the anticipation quiver down the length of her legs.

The crop fell against her buttocks once more, raining an agonizing yet endurable pain, but she continued to fondle herself. It was unlike anything she had ever experienced. The pleasure. The pain. One seemed to fuel the other. The agitation blazing in her body was ten times stronger than what she had felt earlier. She did not care if he ordered her to stop this time. She would not do it. Her body deserved to spend this time.

And spend it did. She jerked against the post as her wave crested, rolling her beneath it, into the glorious turbulence of release. It flared deep in her groin, shot down her legs. A wrenching cry tore from her throat. When at last she surfaced for air, she felt weak and ragged. Her legs collapsed beneath her just as he swept her into his arms and undid the last of the bonds. He tossed aside the bodice of her gown and laid her across the bed.

With her eyes closed to contain the intensity of sensations that had just assaulted her, she breathed in the relief of her accomplishment, her body satisfied and content despite the ache in her limbs and the tingling of her buttocks. His hand caressed the welts on her arse with a gentleness she would not have thought possible given how forcefully he had wielded the crop. She felt something cool and moist—a salve of some sort—applied to her. It eased the burn and soothed the ache.

"You did well, Heloise."

"Mmmmm," she acknowledged, relishing the sound of her name upon his tongue.

She thought he might now put his triumph into words, and she would not have cared much if he did. Lord Blythe had known somehow that she had wanted this. To attempt denials now would prove a futile exercise. But he said nothing. Instead of proclaiming victory—she expected some level of smugness from a man as arrogant as he—he had praised her. She felt proud of herself. Her body had been pushed to limits she had not thought possible. And it felt magnificent.

His gentle rubbing lulled into her a state of peaceful bliss but a gradual arousal also began to build. She could feel the curve of his body behind hers. She was becoming sensitized to his touch in the most alarming and thrilling ways. How was it he could awaken her body with the simplest of caresses? Wetness pooled between her legs once again, desire welling in her veins. She hoped that he would touch her more intimately.

Just as she was about to beg him, his hand circled around her thigh, grazed the soft curls at her mons, and reached for the supple folds of her quim. She could hardly wait to see what he would do next.

SEBASTIAN WAS NOT SURPRISED AT how well Miss Merrill had handled the crop. Wild thoughts ran through his head at the possibilities. There was so much he could do to her. So much he wanted to do to her besides fuck her against the post. How exquisite she would look with her entire body bound in ropes— her arms pinioned behind her, her calves tied to her thighs, her breasts captured and squeezed. Thus tied, she could learn to take him into her mouth and down her throat. It would not be easy, but with the proper incentive, he was confident she was not the sort to give up easily. The vision of his cock gliding between those plump, tender lips was nearly his undoing.

Containing the force of his lust had been like pushing a coach and four up a steep slope, but after she had finished convulsing against the post, when he knew the soreness in her limbs would come alive with a vengeance, a flood of tenderness had filled him. The sense of satisfaction as he cradled her in his arms was greater than he could ever remember it being. He knew not why he felt such a strong desire to protect her. And claim her as his.

Marguerite had been surprised by Miss Merrill, but no more surprised than he. He had taken dozens of women far comelier and more practiced than Miss Merrill. How was it then that he felt driven to madness by her? A cautionary bell rang in his head, one that questioned the wisdom of pursuing anything further.

Her arse had an alluring glow of rose about it. Ignoring the bell, he palmed her buttock and wondered if she was still a virgin here. Marguerite was correct—he didn't do virgins. But hers was such a delectable arse, he found himself considering the prospect, intrigued at being the first to plumb her nether hole. His cock swelled its support for the idea.

Her coiffure had mostly come undone, and tendrils of hair curled about her face and down her neck. Tiny beads of perspiration dotted her nose. He liked her look of disarray. Liked that he was the one who had placed her in such a state. The flush in her rounded cheeks added to her loveliness. His hand wound its way to her mons, brushing her curls and feeling for the dampness between her thighs. A soft moan escaped her lips when he brushed past her clitoris.

He nibbled her ear. "Tell me now, Heloise, how you enjoyed your submission."

"I suppose rather well," she murmured.

Impudent chit, Sebastian thought to himself. He plunged his fingers into her wet folds and jarred them against a raised area of nerves.

"Ahhh," she gasped.

"Only 'rather well'?"

"Extremely well—much—I much enjoyed it."

That is better. He pressed his groin against her buttocks as his fingers continued their assault. She arched herself into his hands.

"Do you desire more, Miss Merrill?"

She paused but a second before nodding her head affirmatively.

"Say it."

"I wish for more."

"More what?"

"More of what you would do to me, my lord."

"Do you wish me to frig you with my fingers?"

"Mmmm."

"Fuck you with my cock?"

Her eyes flew open. Lust smoldered in her countenance.

"Yes, fuck me," she declared in no uncertain terms.

This time it was he who groaned. With one hand still trapped between her thighs, he tore the buttons of his pants loose with the other. His erection sprang out, famished for contact. Too impatient to pull his breeches down, he glided his cock between her legs from behind, then slid an arm beneath her.

He reminded her, "If you wish to put a stop to this, you must utter the word Ma—"

"Yes, yes," she interrupted. "Be a gentleman and pray do not keep a lady waiting."

He ought to punish her for her audacity, but he hungered too much for her at the moment. Without ceremony, he plunged himself into her. It was the best alternative to a sound punishment. She cried out in shock as most, but not all, of his length filled her. Sebastian closed his eyes and took in a deep breath, longing to push himself deeper but wanting her to adjust to the sudden invasion. He knew not how long it had been since last she had been filled. His fingers played her clitoris while the other hand grabbed a breast.

She flexed against his cock. He sank himself deeper into her wet and glorious heat. Suddenly, it wasn't enough for him to be pulsing deep inside her cunny. An insatiable desire to have his body completely merged with hers took hold. He grabbed her chin and turned her mouth toward his, then clamped his lips to hers. At last. How supple, how yielding her lips felt. And he plumbed the depths of her mouth as vigorously as he would plumb the depths of her quim.

She attempted to return his kiss, but he was too busy tasting her, feeling her with his tongue, taking in her air, breathing in her essence. His mouth worked her over, and he felt a rush of her hot liquid encasing his cock. When he finally pulled his mouth from hers, her breath was heavy and she looked dazed. Perhaps he had been a little too fierce in his kiss. He knew not the source of this unexpected ferocity, but he had to sample her mouth once more.

Muffling whatever she was about to say, he pressed his mouth hard to hers. He kissed and sucked her until her lips swelled with lust and the lines of her mouth flushed from the attention. It was maddening, this dueling desire between his mouth and his cock. But the grinding of her hips against him recalled the arousal between his legs. Slowly, he pulled his cock out. She moaned as his shaft grazed her engorged clitoris. He plunged back into her and closed his eyes to concentrate. His sac boiled, greedy for release. A tremor threatened the control of his legs.

She let out a delicious cry as he plunged himself back in. He returned a hand between her legs and began a rhythmic thrusting.

"Oh, *God*," she pleaded, circling her arms behind her and wrapping them about his neck.

A mirror strategically placed opposite them showed two bodies, one darker than the other, writhing in unison, their purpose common. The light of the candles flickered a warm inviting glow upon her milky skin. Her tousled hair was damp about her face from perspiration. He saw his hand fondling her breast. Despite the hardness of her nipples, her areolas remained large, dark discs. He captured the vision of her, of them, in his mind. The image fueled the rage in his cock, and he began to pound her as his fingers plied her with increasing energy and speed.

"Oh God, oh God, oh God," she cried before a scream split their grunting sounds and her body spasmed violently against him.

He continued to piston in and out of her until he had wrung the last of her orgasm out of her. And then he succumbed to the needs of his own body. The scalding desire roiling in his abdomen exploded out his cock, blending into her wetness. With a roar he pumped himself into her. Her body was his. Meant to serve his desires now.

Tremors shot down his legs as his climax peaked. He did not realize how hard he was squeezing her breast until she cried out. He let go and wrapped her in his arms as his lust finished draining into her. The blood pounded relentlessly in his head, but he managed to kiss her gently on the temple. She nestled closer to him. This too was glorious.

And as he cradled her in his arms, he found himself wishing

that what she had said was true. He wished he was indeed devoid
of morals.

Chapter Three

HELOISE AWOKE TO FIND LORD Blythe gone. At first his disappearance did not trouble her. The pleasure of her experience still lingered and as she stretched her arms overhead, she recalled as much as she could, not wanting her memory to forget the smallest detail. Strange as it seemed, it was not merely the havoc he had wreaked upon her body—she had never thought her body could react as intensely as it had—that she cherished the most. The overwhelming sense of freedom, of trust, was what had elevated her experience to the heavens.

She also recalled with fondness their dialogue. That was how he had seduced her. Despite her belief that his philosophy was self-serving—it had to be, for how could someone genuinely believe such radical liberalism? —she had found their conversation stimulating. And he seemed perfectly at ease having such a discussion with her when others would have scoffed at her as some blue stocking. Thus, she did not mind that he might have proved her a hypocrite. She would be more than content to have him prove the point over and over again.

The yearning between her legs began to simmer at the thought. Looking about the room, she wondered what else he might have in store for her. Would he try the nine-of-tails next? Stirring in the bed, she relished the tenderness of her bottom and the ache between her legs, wondering how much more she could take.

The thought frightened and intrigued her.

Annabelle appeared at the door with a tray. "His Lordship asked me to bring some victuals."

Eying the thinly sliced ham and colorful sweetmeats, Heloise realized she was famished. Annabelle set the tray upon the bed and poured a glass of wine.

"Your gown is being ironed, madam," Annabelle said, "and I shall return shortly to attend to your toilette."

"Thank you."

After a quick bob, the maid left. As Heloise buttered her bread, she wondered why she should bother getting dressed if she would end up naked again. Oh, but the process of undressing was delightful. She wondered if she would have the opportunity to see him completely naked. The thought made her salivate more than the food.

"The berries are fresh from the garden."

She glanced quickly to the door. The Earl of Blythe stood on the threshold, dressed magnificently in gray. She had never found gray to be an appealing color, but he wore it well. The hue would have made a pale man look ashen but did nothing to tarnish the bronze in Lord Blythe's complexion. He wore his riding hat and riding boots and a light cloak was draped about his shoulders.

"Are you headed out?" she asked. She glanced out the windows to see that the sun had just begun to emerge from the horizon.

"If you leave within the hour, you will be home not long after dawn," he informed her.

Her brows lifted in reaction—she had not even been here a day—but the tone of his voice suggested he had no interest in prolonging her stay. What had happened? Had she done something to offend? She had thought he approved of her performance. Was that not so?

"You're letting me go?" she asked.

"It was never my intention to keep you prisoner. I may be devoid of morals, but I am no tyrant."

Never his intention or not his desire? Would he have felt differently if she were Josephine?

"What of Josephine?" she inquired when he touched his hat to her and prepared to take his leave.

"You may rest easy, Miss Merrill. I will not be extending another invitation to your cousin."

Because he might end up with her instead? She watched him depart in stunned silence. Was this how he was with the other women? Did he bring them ecstasy, show them a bit of affection, then cast them aside as quickly as possible?

Of course. What a fool she had been to think that he might have taken a fancy to her. Apparently she did not merit even a full weekend with him. He had proved his point and shown her for a charlatan. Did she expect anything else from entangling herself with a rake like Sebastian Cadwell?

The bread, though freshly baked, suddenly tasted stale to her. With a sigh, she pushed away the tray and rose from the bed to prepare for a long and lonely journey home.

*　＊　＊*

"SURELY YOU ARE NOT LEAVING so soon, *mon cheri?*" Lady Follet asked from the settee where she lounged in a stola.

Sebastian bowed. "I have no reason to stay, and came only to bid you *adieu.*"

"*Adieu?* But why?" Marguerite persisted as she plucked a grape off its stem.

He eyed the two brawny men, dressed in togas, who had been servicing her. "I have no wish to trouble you with more than a goodbye, seeing as you are occupied, my lady."

She waved her pair of Adonises away. "I am now *unoccupied.*"

"Nevertheless, I intend a brief farewell."

Marguerite pursed her lips in a pout. He could not help but compare her wide and thin lips with those of Miss Merrill's. Parting from Miss Merrill had proved more difficult than he had anticipated—especially as she sat naked in that bed, ready to be taken again. He had considered fucking her one last time, but that would only have delayed the inevitable awkwardness. And he had had a hard enough time looking into her eyes after what had transpired between them.

"Ah, you offended your lady friend in some manner and she is leaving in a huff," Marguerite noted. "You will, of course, give chase, prove that she cannot resist you, and fuck her madly in your carriage."

He swallowed hard, trying not to imagine the scene being played out with Heloise—Miss Merrill.

"I am sending her away," he explained.

"But why?"

"Because she came in error. She is not suited for Château Follet."

"Her cries would indicate otherwise. She was enjoying herself—my servants told me they could hear her from down the hall. And, regardless of what Anne Wesley would say, no woman has been known to be dissatisfied in your hands."

Sebastian let out an impatient breath through his nose. He had little desire to discuss the matter with Marguerite, but she was the hostess, and his manners would not allow him to dismiss her easily.

"The misgivings lie with me."

"She displeased you."

He wished that were the case. He wished that he had not found her courage and attempts at boldness endearing. Nor her vulnerability so alluring. Her body so intoxicating.

"She pleased me well enough."

Marguerite arched her brows. "Pray tell you are not developing a conscience, *mon cheri?*"

Women. They could be damnably clever at the most inconvenient times.

"She would not think it possible," he replied wryly, "having denounced me as a libertine devoid of morals."

"But why would she…? Strange words for a woman who came here to experience the pleasures of the flesh."

Sebastian could see Marguerite would not relent until she understood the situation. Only women had such propensities.

"She did not come here to indulge her carnal desires," he

divulged, "but to rescue her cousin from ruin at my hands. Her cousin was my intended guest."

"*Mon dieu.* She took her cousin's place? What a peculiar mademoiselle."

He took this opportunity to raise her hand to his lips. "And now, my dear, I bid you a fond farewell, until next we meet."

She pulled her hand away before he could kiss it. "But you—you seduced her?"

He felt a muscle ripple along his jaw. "My dear, I see no purpose in furthering this *tête-à-tête*. My horse has been saddled."

He turned to leave but was stopped again by her words.

"But why stop now? Why send her away? Does she want to leave?"

"Why so many questions about her?" he retorted. "Why, of the many women who have been through Château Follet, does she merit such curiosity?"

"Because she's not like the many women who have been here. At least not the ones you have brought."

"I did not bring her. She came uninvited."

"Nonetheless, you enjoyed her, did you not?"

Hostess or no, Lady Follet was about to have a rude guest on her hands, he thought to himself.

"It makes little sense that you are sending her away so soon," Marguerite continued, "lest it be an act of conscience, of some form of chivalry. And so, my dear Sebastian, I may ask of you— why her?"

"She is no jezebel. She deserves better."

She stared blankly at him, and he thought that he might finally have put an end to the conversation, but then she began to laugh. Containing his irritation, he waited patiently for her to be done with the hilarity.

"Forgive me," she said at last, wiping away a tear. "I never would have thought to hear you utter such things, but I rather suspected that the day would come when a woman would stir the tender part of you."

The choice of weapon for women was words, and Marguerite,

like Miss Merrill, would have done as well had she kicked him in the groin.

"I am pleased to be a source of humor for you, my dear, but I fail to see where this dialogue is headed."

"*Mon dieu*, I have never seen you this cross. This mademoiselle must be *très special*, indeed. I must meet her."

He took a step toward her. "You will not."

Her brows shot up. "How protective we are. Tell me, she did not ask for you to send her away?"

"It matters not."

"Of course it does. You said she deserved better. What if she doesn't want better—at the least, not your patronizing definition of what is better for her."

He considered Marguerite's words and tried to recall Miss Merrill's reaction upon hearing that she was to return home. He had been so immersed in his own objective that he had not paid much attention to what she might have been thinking.

"It is better that she go," he said at last.

"Coward."

Of all the things Marguerite could have said, he did not expect that. Rather, he had thought she might praise him for his rare display of chivalry with Miss Merrill or chastise him for being a chivalrous prude. Being called a coward was worse than anything Anne Wesley might have said.

"My dear, you are deliberately trying to provoke my ire," he said, taking off his gloves as if he meant to slap her across the face and challenge her to a duel.

She eyed the gloves warily. "Only because I adore you, Sebastian, and only the friendship between us stays the jealousy I feel towards your mademoiselle."

"If you wish to renew our acquaintance, I can have the groom unsaddle my horse."

"No. I will not serve as a means for you to forget *her*. I do not wish for you to envision her while you lie with me. If you are the Sebastian Cadwell I thought you were, you would not let her go."

"How many times do you intend to challenge my manhood,

Marguerite?"

She smiled.

"It would do no good," he said. "If she returns home now, there is a chance no one would find out that she had ever been here. If she stayed, while we might enjoy ourselves for a few days more, we would only defer the misery of parting."

"That has never stopped you before. Is it her misery or yours that concerns you?"

He considered the many women he had bid farewell to. Some parted with wistfulness, others parted with vain attempts to seduce him. But he had been clear with them all—their time at Château Follet marked the end and not the beginning of an affair. He did not think he could bear seeing the sadness in Miss Merrill's eyes. Already he suspected she, like so many before her, had fallen a little in love with him. Nor had he a desire to enlarge the emptiness he was already feeling upon her departure.

"I will not see her ruined," he said stubbornly.

"How condescending of you."

Her words struck him as ironic. He had used the same with Miss Merrill. And now it was he who sought to shield her from herself—contradicting his own arguments. He would have preferred to keep Miss Merrill and show her body the many paths to ecstasy. Instead, he had chosen to be selfless, and for that he was being called a condescending coward.

"Go to her, *mon cheri*," Marguerite urged.

She gazed at him with obvious affection. He wondered if Miss Merrill would gaze at him with such warmth. The prospect beckoned as much as her body called to his.

"*Adieu*, my dear," he said to Marguerite with a kiss to her forehead.

And this time, before she could utter another objection, he took his leave.

H ELOISE HAD THE CARRIAGE DEPOSIT her a mile from the Merrill estate with the intention of traversing the remaining distance on foot. Watching the carriage withdrawing into the sunset, she was poignantly conscious that her assignation with Lord Blythe was over. She might not cross paths again with him for some time, and she would prefer the absence to the inevitable awkwardness that must accompany future encounters between them.

She welcomed the solitary walk, hoping the pleasant glow of dusk would calm her unrest. Cadwell had stirred an agitation within her that she could not quiet. Longing for his touch, her body felt as though it were a tuning fork that could not cease its reverberation. What a muddle she had made of herself! Though driven by good intentions, she had succeeded in accomplishing nothing save making a proper fool of herself before the Earl of Blythe. Her cheeks flushed at what he must think of her now.

The most troubling aspect of it all was that she cared what he thought.

As she approached the house, her thoughts turned to Josephine and the dreaded confrontation. How would she explain herself to her cousin? She had reconciled herself to the prospect of losing Josephine's affection in exchange for "rescuing" her cousin from Lord Blythe, but now that her mission had proved a failure—and that she herself had succumbed to that from which she had sought to protect Josephine—she no longer felt secure in her standing.

"Miss Merrill!" the maidservant at the door greeted her in surprise, louder than Heloise would have liked. "We was in quite a state as to where you might have gone off to."

"I went to call upon an ailing friend," Heloise mumbled as she glanced about for her cousin with a quickened pulse. "Where is Miss Josephine?"

"In the garden, I believe, with Mr. Webster."

Mr. Webster was a friend of Lord Blythe and had called once before on Josephine.

"Is anyone else with them?"

The maid shook her head. Heloise sighed at Josephine's disregard for a chaperone, but she was relieved too, that she might not have to confront her cousin quite yet.

"Shall I assist in your toilette, Miss Merrill?"

With her skirts dust-covered from the walk, Heloise realized she must have looked rather unkempt from her travels. They went upstairs to her chambers, which now looked a tad drab compared to those at the Château Follet.

As she unlaced her bonnet and shrugged out of her caraco, she thought once again of Lord Blythe, of his hands undressing her, his body pressed against her. How quickly her apprehension had transformed to comfort in his presence, as if they had been lovers for some time. She would never have imagined that she could experience such ease with a man and that the words "fuck me" would fall from her lips as effortlessly as a comment about the weather.

"Allow me."

Heloise whirled around. She had stepped out of her skirts and awaited the maid to unlace her stays when Josephine appeared. Her breath stalled.

Josephine pulled at the ribbons without word. The frown upon her lips and the stiffness of her hand revealed her displeasure. "You know?" Heloise ventured.

"I was awaiting the invitation. When none arrived and I discovered you absent without any of the servants knowing your whereabouts, I suspected your interference."

She forced a breath. "Forgive me, Josephine."

Josephine paused before replying, her voice quavering with anger, "You are not my keeper, Heloise."

Heloise stared at the floor. "I know. I was wrong to have intervened. I should not censure you were you to decide never to speak to me again."

"Then why did you?" her cousin accused.

Noble if not condescending sentiments, the earl had said.

Heloise took a deep breath and looked into Josephine's eyes. "I was a fool."

With an exasperated sigh, Josephine flopped into an armchair nearby. "You went all the way to Château Follet?"

She nodded.

"And spoke with Lord Blythe?"

"Yes."

"What did you say to him?"

"I beseeched him not to besmirch your honor."

Josephine snorted. "What did he say?"

"That I was intolerant and that you were not in leading strings."

Her cousin pursed her lips as silence fell between them. Heloise had stepped out of her stays and clasped her hands together. She had prepared herself for Josephine's wrath and was ready to receive it.

"That is not your chemise," Josephine observed with narrowed eyes.

Heloise eyed the undergarment with its lace edging. It was more exquisite than any she owned and belonged to Lady Follet. However, Lady Follet had a slender figure and the chemise stretched visibly over Heloise's body. She searched her mind for a reasonable explanation but contrived nothing. Now Josephine would be livid...

"What happened at the château, Heloise?"

Her mouth opened, but no words emerged. Helpless and embarrassed, she could only look at Josephine stupidly.

"Heloise, did you and Lord Blythe...?"

She dropped her gaze and felt her cheeks redden.

Josephine shook her head. "That rake! I wonder that he accepted you for a replacement?"

Heloise looked at her cousin. "I am sure he was exceedingly disappointed."

Silence. Then a sly smile pulled at the corner of Josephine's mouth. "Well, Heloise. I must say that such display of boldness on your part is quite surprising!"

"I will no longer attempt to thwart your acquaintance with him," Heloise assured her.

Josephine sniffed. "Indeed! Imagine what would be said of you if it should be discovered you spent the night at Château Follet. I think you shall no longer lord over me simply because you are my senior. But did Lord Blythe make mention of when he would repair my stolen invitation?"

A shameful seed of jealousy threatened to sprout, but Heloise suppressed the feeling. "He did not."

Josephine knit her brows for a moment, but then waved a hand dismissively. "The invitation is no great loss, though admittedly, I was quite furious when it dawned on me what you had done. But if the Earl of Blythe will not replicate the invitation to Château Follet, *Mr. Webster* will."

Heloise said nothing.

"Tell me, is Lord Blythe as divine as rumored?"

And more, Heloise thought. She noted the mischievous sparkle in her cousin's eye.

"He is!" Josephine exclaimed. "For you are blushing as scarlet as a pimpernel."

"Only because I have made a royal fool of myself. He proved me for a hypocrite."

"I own it is a relief to find you are not quite so virtuous. It is rather taxing to think that I am somehow short of character when compared to you."

Heloise let out a shaky breath. "I think that I owe you my confidence, dear cousin, but I was compromised long before this."

Josephine's eyes turned into saucers.

"Of my own volition," Heloise added. "Perhaps that is why I thought it no large matter to…to lie with Lord Blythe."

"And I had been led to believe you were the virtuous one!"

"When your father was kind enough to take me in, I vowed I would not bring shame upon him—or you, Josephine. You are my only family and far too dear to me."

"But you ought not advise me to adhere to expectations you yourself have not fulfilled."

"Your prospects, Josephine, are much greater than mine."

"Yes, yes, but it is so much more pleasurable to succumb."

Heloise sighed in agreement. She sat down on the bed, and the two shared a moment of silence.

"There is no purpose in protecting me, Heloise. I had surrendered my maidenhead a year ago."

Now it was Heloise's turn to be surprised. "Of your own volition? Did you consider the consequences?"

"Did you?" Josephine retorted.

"Touché."

"Where is the harm if no one knows?"

"I wish we had shared our confidences earlier. Perhaps all this could have been avoided."

"Perhaps. But then you would not have experienced the embrace of Lord Blythe."

Heloise thought of the desire that had been stoked to life by the earl. The hunger had lain dormant these years—suppressed—and she had lamented its awakening at first. But perhaps she could exalt in its vigor instead? Why should the thrill of it turn sour simply because she could not be with Lord Blythe?

Looking at her cousin, she saw that Josephine's countenance had softened. "I hope that someday you may forgive me, Josephine."

"I may be cross with you still," Josephine said, but a faint smile tugged at one corner of her lips. "But I do prefer the Heloise I know now."

Heloise felt as if a boa had loosened its hold of her chest.

Josephine leaned in. "Now tell me *everything* about the Château Follet…"

CLOSING HIS EYES, SEBASTIAN IMAGINED the plush lips of Heloise Merrill wrapped about his cock, the look of lust shimmering in her eyes as he pushed his erection deeper into her mouth. He had bound her arms behind her to call more attention to her breasts. Naked and upon her knees, she was far too delectable a vision not to fuck. The only dilemma was which orifice to take first. But he had taken notice of her mouth ever since their encounter at the theater, when her bottom lip had dropped in astonishment over something he had said. He had been tempted then to run his thumb over her succulent lips.

Her mouth, a rose to be plundered by his cock, willingly took in his thickness. He sawed his cock in and out of her, felt the velvet of her tongue grazing his length, throbbed when she sucked the crown of his penis. Was there a heaven greater than that of her moist warmth encasing him? Wrapping a hand behind her head, he pushed her further onto his cock until his tip brushed the back of her throat. She gagged at first but relaxed when he rubbed the base of her head. Soon her lips were touching the hairs of his pelvis, her chin pressed against his scrotum. A few more thrusts and the fire in his blood, the roiling in his sac could not be contained.

The stream of his desire shot from his cock as the screams of the woman beneath him jolted him from his reverie.

He climbed off her before the last of his seed had emptied. Stumbling, he leaned against the wall for support and took in a deep breath. He was not in the Empress Room of Château Follet but the boudoir of an opera dancer, and the woman sprawled upon the bed with her skirts thrown above her waist was not Miss Merrill but a woman whose name he could barely recall. Three days had passed since he had left the château and still he could not quiet the humming in his body whenever he thought of Miss Merrill. Perhaps he should not have dismissed her quite so soon from Château Follet. There was much he wanted to show her, much he wanted to do with her body. Would she enjoy being bent over the back of a chair, tied to the posts of the bed, or suspended in bondage? He wondered which position he would most favor with her—throwing her legs over his shoulders, pressing her against the wall, or taking her from behind as she knelt on all fours?

The answer would surely prove to be *all of them*.

Despite having just spent, he felt desire welling once more in his groin. He glanced at the woman, now asleep, in the bed before him. For a moment he considered climbing back onto her, but she looked far too tranquil in her slumber, and he suspected that pounding himself senselessly into her would not dispel his thoughts of Miss Merrill.

An hour later he found himself at Brooks's, but neither cards nor drink proved an effective distraction. He longed not only for her body but her company. There was so little he knew of her, save that Jonathan Merrill had become her guardian upon the

death of her parents. He wanted to know what she thought of
Château Follet after her experience with him? He would like to
believe that he had surpassed the depths of any encounters she
had had with previous lovers.

"*Go to her,*" Marguerite had urged.

He imagined the possibilities of a second encounter with Miss
Merrill. The grounds of the château possessed a bucolic charm,
and he would have liked to take her on a stroll and engage her in
a less confrontational situation. He sensed that he could speak to
her as a peer and on a world of topics. Some women had a most
annoying practice of feigning ignorance or appearing stupid to
please the vanity of the men in their company, but Heloise was
as likely to challenge him. Of course he could always silence any
argument from her by smothering her mouth with his own.

A second assignation would provide him an opportunity to
make amends for his abrupt departure from her. The look of
surprise, the slight frown of her brows had indicated her disappointment when he had taken his leave. He had no doubt she had
the fortitude to recover, though he half wished, selfishly, that her
recovery would not be too swift. He wondered if he occupied
her thoughts as much as she did his. He hoped, for her sake, that
it would not be the case. Or did he?

He shook his head. He had denied his lust in favor of honor. To
seek another meeting with Heloise would tarnish the integrity
of his *noblesse oblige.* There were others more suited to Château
Follet. Perhaps he could amuse himself by seducing Anne Wesley
into retracting her unkind words. He was confident she would
sing his praises before long.

Time would ensure that Miss Merrill became but a faint memory. If only that were what he desired.

THE WEEDS RESISTED, AND HELOISE welcomed their
defiance as she tugged at them—anything to command her
attention and keep her mind off Château Follet and the Earl of
Blythe. A sennight had passed and still it was no easy matter to forget him, especially in the quiet of night. Lying in bed, she would

caress the parts of her that he had caressed. Her body longed for his touch and the way he made her feel alive. She missed their exchanges.

But she had not heard from him since leaving Château Follet. She knew not if he had attempted to contact Josephine. Somehow she suspected he was done with both Miss Merrill as well as Miss Josephine.

The afternoon sun shone brightly and perspiration trickled down the side of her face as her uncle approached her. He looked very much like her father, only a bit more stout about the belly. She often thought how fortunate she was that she had such a kindhearted guardian.

"Er, Heloise," he said, peering at her through his bifocals. He hesitated, apparently deciding not to say what he had initially intended.

Ceasing her activity, Heloise looked up at him and waited.

After clearing his throat a few times, her uncle blurted, "How do you know the Earl of Blythe?"

Heloise felt her stomach drop. "Sir?"

"He is not a man I thought would be familiar to you."

Avoiding his gaze, Heloise wondered how she could answer him. This was not how she had meant to repay his kindness for taking her in, and yet she was guilty of deception and shame. Should she confess the whole truth and offer to take her leave? Surely he would not want to keep her in his household after learning the truth?

"He has a…" her uncle began again, "a repute of sorts, you know."

"Yes, I am aware of his character," she replied, fidgeting with her gloves. She dug for courage to ask, "Why do you wish to speak of Lord Blythe?"

"He is here."

Her breath halted sharply. "He—Lord Blythe came to see you?"

"He came not for me but for you."

"Me?" she echoed. "Not…Josephine?"

"I, er, asked the same, but he was quite clear. A direct man, this earl. In truth, his candor took me by surprise. Nonetheless, I told him that I would not be deemed a responsible guardian if I were to countenance your acquaintance with him. He said he quite understood my fear that I would be feeding the sheep to the wolf, as it were, but he praised your sense of judgment, and I had to agree. I do wish Josephine shared of your discrimination."

The irony of his words made her cringe.

"I leave it up to you then," he continued, "to decide if you will see him. If you've no wish to, I will send him away."

Heloise searched his face and realized there was no anger there. "I will see him."

When her uncle left, she wished she had asked him to make the earl wait in the drawing room, that she might have an opportunity to attend her toilette. Having exerted some effort in gardening, she must have looked as unkempt as she had that first day at Madame Follet's. She removed her gloves, wiped the perspiration from her brow, and attempted to tuck her curls into some sense of order.

But why worry of her appearance? she reasoned to herself. She knew not the purpose of his call. Indeed, she had not expected to see him again after his departure from the château. But perhaps he harbored some guilt for having seduced her? Or wished to point out that he had not seduced her but that she had willingly given herself to him so that she had no claims upon his conscience? Perhaps he wished once more to warn her not to meddle in his affairs. Well, she had no intention of interfering in his pursuit of her cousin. And she had no wish to force his hand. No one knew she was ruined, and she trusted him not to speak of it. Though she had not been able to refrain from thinking of him these past days, he would not know it.

Still, she could not stay her vanity from smoothing down her gown and being dismayed upon discovering a stain. She tried to rub it out.

"Miss Merrill."

Her head snapped up to see the Earl of Blythe standing before her, as immaculately dressed as ever in his high polished Hessians, trim cutaway coat with brass buttons and starched cravat.

"Your lordship," Heloise returned as blandly as she could, attempting not to be unnerved by the manner in which his gaze bored into her as she bobbed a curtsy.

Silence settled between them as he took her in. Heloise pulled at the fingers of her gloves. It was he who had called upon her. Why did he not speak? Afraid that he would unearth her true feelings, she kept her eyes averted and waited unsuccessfully for him to begin the dialogue. When he did not, she was tempted to ask him if he had come all this way simply to stare at her.

"You have a purpose for your visit, Lord Blythe?" she relented at last.

He eyed her carefully. "Indeed."

The man was insufferable. He was not making this easy for her.

"My cousin is not here," she informed him, tossing her gloves into a basket with her gardening tools. She was determined that he would not know the pain she had felt when he had left the château with only the slightest by-your-leave. Nor would he know the anger she felt—anger that now fueled her nerves when a part of her wanted only to flee from him that she might shed her tears in solitude.

"I came not for her."

Of course she knew that. Her uncle had said as much. Nonetheless, and though she knew not the purpose of his call, she felt gratified to hear from his own lips that he was here for her, no matter his purpose.

"Then why did you come?" she ventured.

"Our farewell at the château was unsatisfactory," he answered, his voice dark.

Ah. She had suspected he had more compassion than he had shown.

"I found it decent enough," she lied and even managed a small smile at him. Her response seemed to unsettle him, but her triumph was diminished by the wretchedness she felt. She wished he would leave so that she might properly grieve over a romance that lived only in her imagination, berate herself for having been such a dolt, and return to being the sensible young woman her uncle had praised but moments ago. A sensible and wiser woman.

He narrowed his eyes. "It was an abrupt *adieu*."

"It was." She considered as she picked up her basket, proud that she maintained her composure, but she did not trust it to last much longer. "But pray do not trouble yourself on that."

She turned to leave but he grasped her wrist. Her heart hammered violently at his touch.

"Trouble myself?" he said in a near growl. "I have only slept fitfully these last seven nights since leaving you."

For the first time she noticed the darkness beneath his eyes. Had he as strong a conscience as that? Despite her anger at him, her heart ached for his distress.

When he did not release her, she glanced toward the house to see if her uncle might be watching. He would not approve of such familiarity from the earl. Realizing the same, Lord Blythe dropped her wrist—reluctantly, it seemed.

"It were my own fault," he said. "It was not a proper farewell."

Though his jaw was still tight, the look in his eyes had softened. She faltered and could not stop her voice from quavering as she asked, "What…what would you have considered a proper farewell, my lord?"

His gaze made the space about them intimate without his having to stir. His response was low and husky. "Something I dare not do at present, for I would not cause a scandal in your uncle's garden."

She stared at him with her mouth agape. Groaning, he glanced toward the house, then defiantly stepped toward her, placed his finger beneath her chin as he had done that night in the theater, and closed her mouth.

"Your lips will be the death of me, Miss Merrill," he murmured.

The hammering of her heart moved up into her head, making it difficult for her to think. His touch recalled their night of passion, and her body thrilled to it instantly. In his eyes, she now beheld a smoldering agony. Did she dare hope…?

"My lips?"

"Yes. The vision of which has haunted me day and night."

She closed her eyes and heard his words echo in her head. *Haunted me day and night.* Just as he had haunted her thoughts and dreams. The anguish melted from her and with it her calm.

A breeze wafted around them, blowing the scent of the flowers into the air.

As if encouraged by the look in her eyes when she opened them, Sebastian continued, "I came, Miss Merrill, to inform your uncle of my intentions to court you."

Dumbfounded, she could only stare at him. The words he had uttered sounded almost ludicrous. Court her?

"I intend the courtship to bear all the markings of respectability," he assured her, unsettled by her silence, "though, damn me, it will be no easy feat when my body burns with desire for you."

Her mouth fell open again. If her heart could glow, she would be brighter than a beacon. She recovered from the audacity of his statement. "Respectability from you, Lord Blythe?"

"It took me seven days to realize that I have no choice but to attempt respectability if I ever hope to possess you in my arms once more. You deserve no less. But I give you fair warning—you know me for what I am, Miss Merrill."

"I do not think I do," she returned. "I thought our affair confined to the château. Your departure made that quite clear, I think."

"I was appalled," he explained, "that you might be discovered in a compromising situation."

She flushed. "You may recall, sir, that you have not the honor of having been the first."

A muscle rippled along his jaw. "I will not discuss the particulars of *that.* I thought that you would wake with remorse for what had happened betwixt us and that you would be relieved for me to be gone."

"Yet here you are," she pointed out.

"Yes, here am I, for it is the nature of the male sex to pursue, against all odds, until he has been bludgeoned and all recourse dissolved. I want you, Miss Merrill, more than I have ever wanted most other women. If the nature of such feelings should be love,

I will not spurn it."

She contemplated what he said, her gaze raking over him, saying nothing. She felt mastery of the situation, for he had made clear his feelings but she had yet to reveal hers. He was staring at her as if she were prey he meant to devour. Desire lighted his eyes, and the look made her loins warm and a familiar wetness begin to form. But she continued playing the coquette through her silence for well he deserved it.

"You disappointed me, Lord Blythe," she said at last.

His brows rose.

"I had hoped to stay the full three nights at Lady Follet's," she finished.

He beamed.

"As for respectability…" she continued, her eyes bright as she leaned toward him, "that sounds rather boring."

He groaned. "Miss Merrill, you would make a further rake of me."

"There is a part of the garden hidden from all view," she whispered with a sly smile.

"I could not, Miss Merrill," he said after some hesitation. "I may be a rake, but you will not find it so easy to question my resolve as you had. I will be a gentleman."

Not for long, she thought to herself. She had no qualms about seducing him. But she gave him her brightest smile and took the arm he offered to escort her back to the house.

"How unfortunate," she replied lightly, using his words. "Perhaps that can be changed."

The Earl of Blythe grinned. "My dear Miss Merrill, you are a perfect rake."

THE END

Read on for more Chateau Debauchery Adventures…
And if you enjoyed the stories you read, please consider leaving a review.

Excerpt from:

Submitting
TO THE
MARQUESS

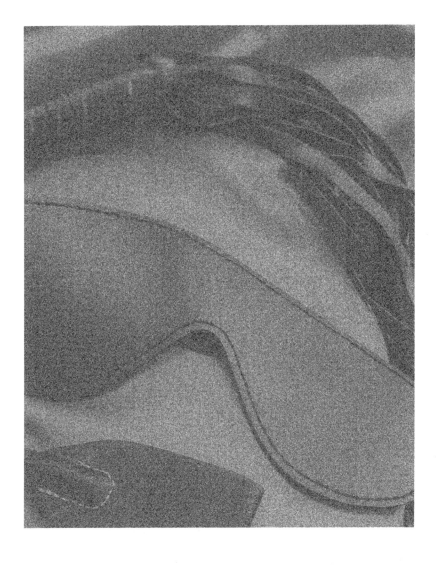

Chapter One

Regency England

"WELL, YOUR WICKED COUSIN DEIGNS to show, does he?" Mrs. Grace Abbott asked of her daughter, Mildred, as she looked across the ballroom at a gentleman who had turned many a head by his appearance.

Knowing the question to be more of a statement, Mildred, a practical young lady of four and twenty, made no reply as she fanned herself to keep from perspiring overmuch, which she was wont to do in crowded spaces, during uncommonly warm summer evenings, whenever she fretted, and if she should have on one too many layers of clothing. All four of these aspects conspired against her tonight, and the moisture would certainly ruin the many applications of powder her mother, declaring that Mildred's complexion showed too darkly in the summer months, had insisted upon.

As the occasion for the ball was Lady Katherine d'Aubigne's fiftieth birthday, Mrs. Abbott had also insisted Mildred wear the shawl that her ladyship, Mrs. Abbott's esteemed sister-in-law, had gifted Mildred last Christmas. Mrs. Abbott never failed to consider how she might curry the favor of her ladyship, the hostess of the evening's soiree.

Mildred adored Lady Katherine, but for once, her attention was more fixed upon her cousin, the Marquess of Alastair. She had hoped he would be in attendance and had thought of little else on the carriage ride over. Yet, now that she beheld his tall and imposing form, her nerves faltered and she wondered that she had the courage to speak to him, though she had never before felt intimidated. She was not one given to asking for favors from anyone, let alone the marquess, but she was in some desperation tonight.

"I heard he had been dallying with some chit from the *bourgeoisie*," Mrs. Abbott continued. "I would have thought, once he had come into the marquessate, that he would forsake his rakish ways. It is a shame, for the former marquess was an upstanding man."

"You ought not speak ill of Alastair, Mama," Mildred said. "He has been quite generous in providing for my dowry."

Mrs. Abbot sniffed. "Well, it was the only proper thing to do as he can well afford it and the two of you are cousins."

Though her mother, whose older brother had married Lady Katherine, needed no reminding, Mildred replied, "Cousins by marriage."

"Cousins, nonetheless."

"The marquess is under no obligation to assist us, even if his aunt married Uncle Richard."

"No obligation? We are family!"

Sensing that her mother was determined to see Andre d'Aubigne, the Marquess of Alastair, in poor light, Mildred offered no further comment. Nothing short of his lordship offering his hand to Mrs. Abbott's daughter would improve Grace's perception of him. If such a miraculous event as a proposal should come to pass, Mrs. Abbott would have gladly forgiven all his imperfections.

"I suppose your father should introduce George to your cousin."

Mildred stiffened at the name of her fiancé, an uninspiring and officious man. But despite their connections to the d'Aubigne family, Mrs. Abbott, being the fourth daughter, and Mr. Abbott, a fifth son with no entailment to speak of, could not be particular. Mildred had had few suitors since her come-out. With a figure slightly plump and a face more round than oval, she had only the brightness of her eyes and the shape of her nose to recommend her countenance.

"I doubt Alastair will stay long enough for introductions," Mildred thought aloud. She knew her cousin favored gaming hells over social gatherings of any sort.

Mrs. Abbott scowled. "Well, I shall have to find your papa and ensure that he introduces George as soon as possible. George is quite eager to meet your cousin."

"Yes, he is," Mildred affirmed. She rather suspected that, if they had not any relation to the d'Aubigne family, George Haversham would not have proposed.

She had made a grievous error in accepting his hand yesterday. The proposal had come as a surprise, and she had convinced herself that she ought not fall into the same habits as her mother in refusing to see the better qualities of a man. She should be grateful that a man had offered for her at all.

But last night, sleep had eluded her. The prospect of marriage, and all the obligations that accompanied that institution, had roused desires that she had worked hard to suppress for the better part of the year. They were desires of such a dark nature that she once thought she had been cursed by the devil. It was shameful enough to find that she had not the fortitude to keep her virtue, but these wicked inclinations of hers horrified even as they titillated.

Her discovery by one she revered had, surprisingly, set her at ease with these disturbing proclivities. Nevertheless, as her parents had grown more anxious regarding her prospects of matrimony, Mildred had resolved to keep her secret wantonness at bay.

But they called to her often.

As the night wore on, she began to consider that spinsterhood did not appear all that unfavorable next to marriage with Haversham. She did not wish to be a burden to her parents, but if she should never marry, she decided that she could find employment as a governess or a lady's companion. Lady Katherine would assist her.

She had first considered appealing to Lady Katherine but

loathed to trouble her ladyship with her woes. As it would be most unseemly for her to call off the engagement, it remained for Haversham to retract his offer or fail to come to terms with the marriage settlement.

For that to happen, she needed Lord Alastair.

As soon as her mother had left in search of her father, Mildred rallied her nerves, dotted her brow with her handkerchief, and prepared to speak to the Marquess. But first, she was beset by three of her peers eager to ask after her cousin.

"Which dance do you think Lord Alastair most partial to? Does he fancy cotillions?" asked Helen.

"Alas, I do not think him partial to dancing of any sort," Mildred replied.

"But he must dance!" remarked Jane. "There is such the shortage of men with so many off to fight Napoleon. It would be so very impolite of him not to dance."

"I think you overestimate my acquaintance with him, but I would hazard that he would wear the label of rudeness as easily as he does the label of rake."

"How is it you are even able to talk to him?" asked Margaret. "He always appears quite put out at being spoken to."

Mildred was tempted to say that the Marquess must feel sorry for her, but he himself would protest that his selfish nature would not accommodate so generous a sentiment as pity.

"Millie, will you not sing my praises to him?" Jane asked. "I *am* your oldest friend. Perhaps you can mention that Henry Westley has taken an interest in me."

"I should be a better friend by *not* calling his attention to you," Mildred replied. "Surely you know his reputation?"

"My brother said the Marquess came very near to a duel once," Helen noted.

"How exciting!" Margaret sighed.

Mildred looked across the room to where Alastair stood talking to his aunt, Lady Katherine. Even without the dash of danger to his character, Mildred understood his appeal. Nearing thirty years of age, his masculinity matured, the Marquess was a handsome specimen of his sex. He enjoyed the sports as much as cards and kept himself in fine physical health. He had the same black hair that all the members of the d'Aubigne family possessed and a smile that could charm when needed. But Mildred found his gaze too sharp and that his lips tended toward a frown.

"He has left a fair number of broken hearts in his wake," she remarked, though she knew full well that nothing called to the fancy of her sex more than the potential reformation of a rake by a woman.

"Surely he will give more thought to marriage now that he is the Marquess," said Jane.

Margaret waved her hand dismissively. "In truth, I simply wish to flirt with the man. That would be plenty exciting for me."

The women giggled in agreement. Mildred smiled. If she had shared their sentiments regarding Alastair, she, too, would have thrilled to receive a smile or a dance from him. Alas, she was to marry George Haversham, and would never know that fluttering of the heart, that spark of excitement, when the object of one's affection comes near. But she was not yet ready to reconcile herself to a life of dullness. She would save herself from such a fate. But she needed the assistance of the Marquess of Alastair.

Chapter Two

H IS LORDSHIP LOOKED AT THE longcase clock on the far wall. Not ten minutes had passed since his arrival. He would stay another twenty minutes before departing for his favorite gaming hell.

"Surely you will give more thought to marriage now," Katherine remarked.

If his aunt persisted on such topics, Alastair resolved he would stay only five minutes more. It was sufficient that he had curtailed his hunting trip to pay his respects to his aunt on her birthday. Aloud, he replied, "And why should you think that, madam?"

"You are the Marquess of Alastair now."

Unimpressed, he said nothing, compelling his aunt to state the obvious.

"You will want an heir."

"If I fail to produce one, the marquessate falls to my uncle."

Katherine wrinkled her nose. "My younger brother is ill prepared to assume the title."

"He is a d'Aubigne. That suffices."

"I suppose if that is your view on the matter, you need never marry."

"I see no reason to add unnecessary concerns to my plate."

"You are fortunate you've no mother to fuss over your unmarried state."

"Do you fret, m'lady?" he asked, for his aunt was as near to a mother as could be had, his own mother having been lost to him when he was a small child.

"I do not. You should know I am *not* the *conventional* sort of woman."

He did indeed know, for it was his aunt who had introduced him to Château Follet, also known as the Château Debauchery, but he raised his brows nonetheless.

"It is not your bachelorhood that concerns me," Katherine continued, "but will you never care for anyone?"

"I protest, madam. I would not be here tonight if I cared for no one. *You* are the reason I am willing to tolerate this tedious evening for any length of time."

"As much as it warms my pride to know that you care for me, I would rather you not confine your affections to me alone. When I am gone, who will be left to care for you?"

He looked down at her ladyship, small in stature but large in heart, and with a willfulness that knew little retreat. "You do fret."

"I suppose I do. Your friends are no friends at all. You have estranged your sisters with your profligacy. You think the rest of the family fools. If you do not find someone to care for, you will die a lonely, miserable old man."

"Madam, there will always be those who care for my title and my wealth. I shall never be lonely."

"Then you will be miserable."

"That I am willing to accept."

Katherine narrowed her eyes. "You think so now because you are at the height of vigor and handsomeness. You will think differently when the wenches are not so readily had."

"Is that why you married?"

"Impudent pup! My dear Richard, God rest him, was the better half of me in every way. I never thought I should find a man who understood me so well. If not for Marguerite Follet, I should never have met my Richard. Perhaps she could recommend a lady for you when you are at her château this week."

He recoiled at the idea. "Madam, I intend to spend my time at

Château Follet suffused in depravity. The only mate I seek is for purely venereal purposes."

He was about to excuse himself and make for the card tables when Mr. Abbott approached with a young man who had styled his hair in long, soft curls, though they did not hide his prominent widow's peak. The many layers of his cravat gave him the appearance of a fancy rooster, and his cutaway coat revealed his large midsection and wide hips to no benefit.

"Lady Katherine, Lord Alastair," Mr. Abbott greeted. "May I introduce to you the gentleman who will be my son-in-law, Mr. George Haversham?"

Katherine held up her quizzing glass, and Alastair knew she was hardly impressed.

Haversham bowed. "A pleasure, Lady Katherine! Many, many happy returns on your birthday. May I compliment you on a delightful soiree? I look forward to the performance of the chamber quartet."

"Son-in-law?" she queried, and despite her poise, Alastair detected a hint of vexation. "When did this happen?"

"Yesterday, my lady, and my happiness is not lessened by the passage of a day," Haversham answered, his silly grin reaching from ear to ear. "Lord Alastair, may I compliment you on your generosity for supplying the dowry for Miss Abbott? Will you be participating in the drafting of the marriage settlements as well?"

"Good God, why would I?" Alastair returned. "Miss Abbott is not my daughter."

Mr. Haversham laughed as if he had been told a droll jest. "No, indeed! I merely thought, as you seem to be quite charitably supportive of your family, that you would extend your interests to all areas of concern. I certainly would not refuse you if and when you saw fit to intervene. Indeed, I should be honored by your involvement."

"My *involvement* extends only so far as providing Mr. Abbott the funds he seeks. What he chooses to do with the monies, even if he should choose to wager it all on horseflesh, is his affair."

Haversham's brow furrowed as he contemplated what it was the

Marquess might be implying.

"I shall be forever indebted to you for your munificence, my lord," Mr. Abbott said.

The marquess expected the man knew better than to comment further or Alastair would be compelled to withdraw his donation. Millie was no dolt, and her intelligence had to come from one of her parents.

"Yes, yes!" Haversham nodded. "We are immensely indebted and exceedingly grateful for your kindness! I cannot give words to express how delighted I am that we shall all be family! Of course, the d'Aubigne name is an illustrious one, whereas I must claim a more humble background, but I think we shall deal well with each other. I should only be too happy to be of service, always, and your humble servant, etcetera."

With a frown, Alastair looked to Abbott to have the sycophant removed.

"Come," Abbott said to Haversham, "I think his lordship and Lady Katherine must have many other guests to greet."

"It was an honor to finally make your acquaintance," Haversham said with a final bow.

When they had left, Katherine turned to her nephew. "My goodness, how much did you promise Abbott?"

"A mere two thousand pounds," Alastair replied. "I thought granting him the sum would spare me his attentions, but I worry that is not to be the case. You had best advise your brother-in-law or I shall rescind my offer."

"I must say that this is perhaps the kindest display of benevolence I have ever seen you make. I am impressed. Perhaps there is hope for you yet."

"Madam, I hope not."

"It is a shame two thousand pounds could not attract better for Millie." Her brow furrowed. "This is all so sudden. I wonder that she did not speak to me of this. I do not think he will suit Millie at all. Not at all. I am rather surprised that Abbott approves of this Haversham fellow. I think her mother and father worry that she will be doomed to spinsterhood if she does not marry soon. Still,

I think they underestimate her qualities."

Alastair suppressed a yawn and glanced once more at the clock.

"It was kind of you to take an interest in your cousin."

Alastair felt the keen eye of his aunt surveying him. "If my giving Abbott two thousand pounds gives me the appearance of altruism or suggests that I give a damn what others are about, then I have made a grievous error. Ah, I see Mr. Priestly is here. He had asked me to invest in the purchase of a racehorse with him. Pray excuse me, madam."

"You will be off soon, I gather?"

"You know me well."

"I intend to travel to Bath within a sennight. I know the fashionable prefer Brighton or Weymouth these days, but the rooms at Bath are still in good shape. I should consider it a fine birthday present if you were to join me."

Alastair suppressed a shudder at taking the waters at Bath. "Recall that I am to spend three days at Château Follet."

"Of course. If I were years younger, I would certainly prefer Château Follet to Bath."

"I had commissioned for your birthday a pianoforte from Vienna. I regret that its delivery has been delayed, but it will have a full six octaves."

"I appreciate the grandeur of such a present, but you need not have. You would make me a happy woman if you granted me something far less impressive but much more meaningful. I would ask nothing more of you if you granted me this one wish."

He raised his brows. "If it is in my power, madam."

"Choose for me one person whose concerns you will take to heart. One person to care for—that is not me. Do this, and I shall even refrain from ever troubling you with talk of marriage and heirs."

He frowned. "Who is to be this person?"

"It is for you to choose. You have many in your family whom could use your protection, guidance and wisdom. I am certain you will make a selection that will make me happy. And this would be the best birthday gift of all to me."

From the corner of his eye, he saw Priestly walking away. "Very well, I will give it consideration."

"Well, do not take forever to make your decision or it will not qualify as a birthday present."

He sensed that Katherine had more to say, but she knew better than to stay him too long. After speaking with Mr. Priestly, he would take his leave. There were too many mothers present who had set their sights upon him, though if they knew what he planned in the way of female companionship this weekend, they would reconsider him as a marital prospect for their daughters. They would be appalled and horrified.

He had not been to Château Follet in some time and looked with anticipation to indulging his most wicked penchants in the coming days.

Chapter Three

MILDRED HESITATED AS SHE OBSERVED her cousin taking his gloves and hat from the groom. He was taking his leave and would not be pleased to tarry. But if she did not speak with him now, she knew not when they would next meet. Resolved, she approached him.

"Alastair, may I have a minute of your time?" she asked, reminding herself that the frown he wore was customary and its cause need not be attributed to her alone.

He turned his dark and penetrating gaze upon her, and, as she had come to stand closer to him than she'd intended, she was quite conscious of how much taller and broader he was than her, though she was no petite maiden.

"My God, you look dreadfully pale, Millie," he drawled in his rich baritone.

A more mannered woman of society might take exception to such a greeting, but Mildred did not mind dispensing with the niceties. "I know it. Mother made me apply at least six coats of powder."

"It looks terrible. I would not recommend it."

"Thank you for your counsel, but I did not come seeking your advice on my toilette. Rather, I had hoped to have a minute with you—"

He raised his brows. "A minute?"

"A few minutes," she corrected as she fiddled with her necklace of pearls. "I know you are eager to attend your gaming hells and will not trespass too much upon your time."

He seemed slightly amused that she knew his destination. "A *few* minutes then, Millie, and only because I know you are economical with your conversation—an uncommon trait in your sex."

"I am much obliged, sir." Feeling the gazes of Helen, Margaret and Jane upon her, she delayed her own purpose for the moment. "I take it you will not stay for the dancing?"

His look of boredom was her answer.

"You would make many a woman happy if you did," Mildred said.

"I would raise many a false expectation," he returned.

"Do you know my friend Jane? I think Henry Westley takes an interest in her—"

"Millie, what is the purpose of our *tête-à-tête?*"

She took a fortifying breath and adjusted her pearls. "I have not had the chance to thank you for providing my dowry."

He groaned. "If I had known my provision would engender such a fuss, I would not have done it."

She perked. "Then don't."

He was taken aback, a rare occasion, for very little surprised or even seemed to interest the marquess. "Don't what?"

"Don't provide for my dowry. I would rather you had not."

He stared at her as if looking for signs of madness.

"I am not yet ready to marry," she explained.

"But it is done. Your father introduced me to your intended tonight."

"And what think you of him, Alastair?"

"You have no wish to know my opinions. They are rarely ever favorable."

"They could not be worse than mine on this matter."

"If you don't like the fellow, why did you accept his hand?"

"Father impressed upon me that I had to. I was overcome, I think, by guilt and a sense of responsibility to my family—I am not you, Alastair. I cannot dismiss what others expect of me."

"I assure you that life is much simpler when you pay others no heed."

"I am quite certain that, without a dowry, Mr. Haversham will lose all interest in me."

His lordship let out a long breath. "Millie, this is not my problem. I have no desire to interfere in your family."

"I am not asking you to speak to father. Simply withdraw the dowry."

"While I may have granted your father his request in a moment of weakness, I will not retract my word. It would not be gentlemanly."

"Since when were you concerned with being a gentleman?" she cried.

He could not resist smiling. When he did, his eyes of grey sparkled. It was what had many a woman undone in his presence.

"Dear Millie, you are far too clever for that Haversham charlatan."

He began putting on his gloves. Seeing that he intended to leave, she suppressed the urge to scowl at him.

"Are you quite certain you wish to invite him into the family?" she tried.

Unperturbed, he donned his hat. "Your few minutes have come to an end. Good night, Millie."

She knew better than to try to stay him. And she was too vexed for words. She should have known Alastair, though he indulged her more than he did most others, would make no effort to come to her aid.

Chapter Four

"OH, LADY KATHERINE, IT IS beautiful!" Mildred remarked as the carriage came into view of the château. Built in the early 18th century and laced with a baroque cornice, the structure had three stories with two pointed towers serving as bookends of the perfectly symmetrical façade. The steep hip roofs of zinc contrasted with the ivory stones. One would have thought the château plucked straight from the French countryside. It stood nestled among mighty oak trees and low verdant hills.

Her ladyship looked out the carriage window with a wistful sigh. "I have not set eyes upon it in many years. Not since Richard passed."

Mildred turned to Lady Katherine. "I cannot thank you enough, my lady, for asking me to join you."

"Careful you do not express too much gratitude or you will sound very much like your betrothed."

Mildred gave a wan smile before sighing. "Yes, though I shall be Mrs. Haversham soon enough."

Her ladyship shuddered. "If you were my child, and I do regard you as such since I have none of my own, I would not permit this marriage to happen. I advised your parents that Mr. Haversham would not suit you, but it appears he is entailed some property, and they feel you will be taken good care of by him. Nonetheless, I had hoped they esteemed me enough to take my recommendation."

"They regard you highly, my lady! But on this, they believe they have the approval of Alastair."

"Hm. And Andre refused your request?'

"He has no wish to concern himself with my troubles."

"Not even for his favorite cousin?"

"I hardly qualify as his *favorite* cousin. I am merely the one who vexes him the least."

"That is no small accomplishment with Andre."

Mildred returned to looking at the château. When Lady Katherine had suggested she take Mildred to Bath with her, Mildred could not have been more thrilled. She did not often travel with her family and had not been to Bath since she was a child. Besides the springs and bath houses, she recalled streets lined with shops, treats of all sorts, and brightly clothed men selling tonics that healed everything from fatigue to warts. But first they would stop to stay a night at Château Follet.

"There is something you should know about the château and its proprietress, Madame Follet," said Lady Katherine.

Mildred gave her ladyship her full attention. There was a peculiar gleam in the woman's eyes.

"It is also known as the 'Château Debauchery.'"

"The Château Debauchery?" Mildred echoed, amused and intrigued.

"The late Monsieur Follet was once imprisoned with the Marquis de Sade and the Comte de Mirabeau."

Mildred's eyes widened. "How wicked."

"Yes, wicked indeed."

"But you say you met Uncle Richard here?"

"I did, but Château Follet is no place for love. It is a place where men and women indulge their most prurient desires, their most naughty and wanton predilections."

Mildred looked carefully at her ladyship to ensure she did not jest, though it did not surprise her that Lady Katherine would speak of such things. The two women had formed an unexpected bond after her ladyship had come across Mildred and a groom in a compromising way in the greenhouse. Mildred had been bent over a table while the groom paddled her backside. Mildred could not have been more mortified, certain she had ruined herself and her family. But, to her great astonishment, Lady Katherine had not castigated her. Instead, she had allowed Mildred to take her into her confidence.

"I shall not commit so dreadful and shameful an act again," Mildred had promised.

"Nonsense, child. You cannot quell the natural desires of your body," Lady Katherine had replied.

Mildred had never been so stunned in her life. Thus began an unusual rapport. Lady Katherine spoke to her of unmentionables, of subjects no proper woman would ever speak, not even to a sister. But Mildred, eager to learn and relieved that her carnal cravings might not be so odd and reprehensible if a woman like Lady Katherine shared in them, drank in every word.

"Is it still known as the Château Debauchery?" Mildred inquired.

"More than ever, I think," her ladyship replied. "I hear the activities have grown darker, more erotic since last I was here."

"And we are to stay here for the night?"

"*You* will stay here. I am far too old for the goings on of the château, and, without Richard, it is not the same. And you will enjoy yourself better without my company."

Mildred stared at Lady Katherine with eyes agog. "You are not staying?"

"Worry not. The guests are most discreet, and Marguerite— Madame Follet, that is—will watch over you. I will speak with her."

"But where will you stay?"

"I've an old friend who lives not far, and I mean to pay her a visit. I will return the morrow to fetch you."

Mildred felt the luster of her prior elation diminish. "I am to be alone at the château?"

"My dear, you are a woman after my own heart. I promise you will have a fine adventure at Château Follet."

"But I know no one. What am I to do?"

"Anything you wish. Madame Follet will acquaint you with all you need know."

"But where shall you stay?"

"An old acquaintance of mine keeps an inn not far from here. I shall pay her and her husband a visit."

Still astonished and now discomfited, Mildred felt her mind in an unsteady whirl. Her ladyship placed a reassuring hand over hers.

"Do not fear, my child. Château Follet is wondrous. If you are to marry that Haversham fellow, you ought to grant yourself one last adventure before you are shackled to the tedium of marriage. Trust me, without Château Follet, as much as I loved your uncle, I wonder that our marriage would have lasted as well."

Mildred did trust Lady Katherine. She admired her ladyship's unabashed honesty of carnal matters and her knowledge of the libidinous. The venereal was the aspect of marriage she most dreaded with Haversham. The man fumbled to kiss her hand and had a painful propensity for planting his foot atop hers whether strolling, dancing or even sitting. How could he possibly fulfill her deepest, darkest cravings?

The opportunity presented to her in Château Follet was rare and special. She pressed Lady Katherine's hand in gratitude.

"I had recommended Château Follet to another before," her ladyship said. "It did not disappoint. I think you will have a most memorable stay. Be free. Be bold. Be wanton."

Mildred glanced out the window and saw that they were about to draw up to Château Follet. It was a little petrifying, but she felt her excitement return. Even greater than before.

WITH EQUAL PARTS APPREHENSION AND anticipation, Mildred followed Madame Follet through the Château. Madame Follet, though several years older, possessed a youthful vibrancy. Mildred had taken to her in an instant and felt she would have done so even if Lady Katherine had not extolled her friendship with the woman. Madame was one of those fortunate women whose beauty did not fade easily with youth. She was much what Mildred was not: stylish in her turban and Turk-ish shawl, fair in countenance and hair, and slender everywhere from her neck to her fingers. In contrast, Mildred had dark locks, almost as black as the d'Aubigne tresses, and a cherubic face.

"I have the perfect room for you here in the west wing," said Madame as they continued down the corridor. "Some guests are staying in the east wing, but as you are new here, I would confine myself to this portion of the Château. The east wing is for the more experienced participants."

Mildred wondered how Madame defined "experienced." They passed by a room with an open door, and Mildred thought she saw a couple, both only partially dressed, upon the bed kissing.

Noticing the look of surprise, Madame smiled. "Some guests do not mind if others watch and observe."

"Truly?"

This was beyond anything Mildred had considered. It was… provocative.

"Would you like to watch?"

Her breath caught. "Pardon?"

"Being a *voyeur* can be quite titillating."

Mildred hesitated. She had not been here above an hour and had not thought to be thrown into the activities already. She had thought she would have more time to adjust to her surroundings, though she knew not how one would prepare for a place like the Château Follet. For certain, watching another couple in congress was extremely naughty. But her response came far more easily than she expected.

"Yes."

Turning around, they went back and stood at threshold of the couple's room. The woman, dressed only in her shift and stays, was lying upon the bed. The man, in only his shirt, hovered above her, kissing her lips, her throat, the top of her bosom. The woman arched her back, trying to press her body closer to his.

"Pray, tease me no longer. I must have you," she murmured.

Mildred stood as still and as quiet as she could, hoping they would not notice her. Her mind screamed that what she did was wrong. Nevertheless, warmth stirred in her belly.

The man straddled the woman, laying his hips over hers. There was a familiar thrusting motion, a sigh from the woman. Mildred felt the heat travel up her cheeks. Was she truly watching this? The man rolled his hips at the woman, who grasped his arms and alternated between grunting and gasping. Their brows furrowed, their cheeks flushed. A mix of emotions churned inside Mildred. She knew their pleasure, knew the corporal cravings that were being simultaneously stoked and satisfied. Thus, she felt as if she were sharing in their interaction. It was naughty to bear witness to such an intimate act, but it was a titillating sight.

The woman's gasps quickened, as did his grunting. His hips hammered into her ferociously. She gave a gasping cry. Seconds later, he roared as he spent before collapsing atop her. They lay, still entwined, breathing hard, their mission complete. Mildred did not move, but she did not know if she ought to stay. For certain, if they saw her, her face would ripen into a tomato.

Sensing her unease, Madame quietly withdrew and Mildred followed. They continued down the corridor. Mildred was silent as she tried to calm the tumult inside her. She had enjoyed the scene, had envied the woman upon the bed. Would she herself ever be so bold?

"You are much like Lady Katherine," Madame said. "She, too, is possessed of an adventurous spirit."

Glancing at Madame, Mildred was filled with a sort of gratitude. For years, until that fateful encounter with Lady Katherine, she had thought herself a most depraved young woman. She knew no one she could talk to. Nothing seemed to stymie the wicked urges within her—not attending church, not reading the Bible over and over, not filling her days with mundane activities, nothing. It was truly a strange affliction because the satiation of it was ever only temporary. In the quiet of her own chambers, she would attend that craving by hand. But, time and time again, the yearning would return. And when that stable hand had put paddle to rear, it had ignited a perverse but superior excitement. The harder the paddling, the more fulfilling it had been.

"Here are your chambers," Madame said, showing Mildred into a nicely appointed and perfectly respectable anteroom.

No one would suspect anything untoward occurred between its walls. Even the pastoral painting upon the wall, of a woman entertaining the attentions of a man on either side of her, seemed tame. Mildred took in the rose-colored, printed silk and golden candelabras upon the walls, and how the late afternoon sun filled the entire room with light. The mahogany furnishings were finer than any in the Abbott house, but it was the general cheerfulness of the room that Mildred found delightful.

"I thought these chambers would suit you." Madame smiled. "As you have no maid of your own, I will have one of mine attend you. Her name is Bhadra. Supper will be at six o'clock. Till then, you are free to roam the château as if it were your own."

Madame gave her a parting smile. Mildred would have liked her hostess to stay. She would have liked to acquaint herself more with the woman, and how the Château Debauchery had come into being, but she would not keep Madame Follet from the other guests.

Alone, she opened the door to the bedroom to see a beautiful post bed clothed in fine linen. She grazed the back of her hand over the soft bedclothes before sitting down.

"Oh!" she exclaimed upon seeing her reflection in a large gilded looking glass above the fireplace. The glass was tilted toward the bed.

How very lecherous, she thought to herself with a smile. Giddiness percolated. She could hardly believe she was to spend the night here. Alone. A part of her wished Lady Katherine would have stayed but perhaps it was, as her ladyship suggested, better this way. Without reminders of her present life, she might lose herself more readily in the world of Château Follet.

She did worry what would happen if she should somehow be discovered here, but Madame Follet assured her that only the most discreet persons were permitted within the château's walls. Any breach of confidence resulted in a permanent ban, and the guests were too devoted to the freedom and opportunities afforded by

Château Follet to risk expulsion.

"Some guests come as a couple," Madame had explained. "Others may find their partners upon arrival. I have many individuals who are unattached, and I know there will be a gentleman—or lady, if that is your persuasion—who would suit you well."

Mildred was not as confident as Madame Follet, though the hostess had named more men than women. If she were not selected, should she take her leave?

"Nonsense," Lady Katherine had replied. "I do not intend to return to collect you till noon the morrow. And I expect, when I return, to receive a rousing account of your time here."

Mildred was, therefore, stuck. It had even seemed to her that Lady Katherine had been in some hurry to leave the château.

Unbuttoning her spencer, Mildred lay back upon the bed and looked at the painted ceiling. Naked cherubs gazed down at her. Her mind wandered back to that other room, to the man rutting atop the woman. The heat between her legs had not completely dissipated.

Slowly, she pulled up her skirts and reached between her thighs to find that little bud of sensation. Replaying the memory of the couple, she sighed as she stroked herself. Yes, she would have liked to be the woman below his bucking hips.

The sound of the door opening made Mildred jump off the bed.

"Miss Abbott?"

It was the maid. Composing herself, Mildred entered the anteroom to find a lovely young Indian with hair of ebony and large almond-shaped eyes.

"You must be Bhadra."

"Yes, miss. Your effects are being brought—ah, here they are."

A groom came up behind her and set down a trunk and portmanteau. He was rather a handsome fellow, Mildred thought to herself, wondering if the servants took part in the château's activities. If she could not find a partner among the guests...

"Shall I dress you for supper, miss?" Bhadra asked.

Mildred marveled at the peaks and valleys of the maid's intonations as she spoke.

"I've not an impressive wardrobe," Mildred said as Bhadra opened the trunk.

"Fine clothing is hardly necessary here, miss. Some guests go without clothing at all."

Mildred imagined what it might be like to walk about in the buff. She had not the confidence to do such a thing but was impressed there were those who would. She wondered how she would react if she came across a nude? How did one stop oneself from staring?

"Even at supper?" Mildred asked.

"Not the first night, lest Madame requests it so."

Mildred faltered. She could not conceive of sitting down to supper sans clothing. How could one concentrate enough to eat? She hoped Madame would not make such a thing mandatory. Mildred would not mind if others wished to shed their garments, but she had no desire to parade her nakedness. If she had a body worth revealing, she might feel differently. Instead, her thighs were a bit wide in proportion to the rest of her legs, there was a tad too much swell to her belly, and she would have preferred a less buxom bosom.

With Bhadra, she undressed from her traveling clothes and selected her finest muslin for supper, the same dress she had worn for Lady Katherine's soiree. It was a simple gown of white with lace at the hem and a lavender sash. In the spirit of the debauchery, Mildred wore only two layers of petticoat. Bhadra had laced her stays extremely tight and this caused her breasts to swell above the décolletage more than usual.

"Do you wish for powder?" Bhadra asked after finishing the coiffure, leaving a few tendrils to frame the face.

Recalling Alastair's comments from the soiree the other night, Mildred shook her head. After applying rouge to her lips, she looked in the vanity and was pleased with what she saw. She looked as pretty as Mildred Abbott could look.

"Monsieur Laroutte will escort you to supper," Bhadra informed.

"Who is Monsieur Laroutte?"

"Madame Follet's brother."

Monsieur Laroutte was at least ten years Madame's senior, but Mildred found the man captivating. They conversed in French, and by the time they had reached the dining room, Mildred decided she would be quite pleased to be paired with the man. However, after seeing that she was seated at the table, he sat at the end of the table opposite where Madame sat at the head, and began conversing with a superbly dressed gentleman to his left. By the manner in which the two men exchanged glances and leaned toward each other, Mildred wondered if they might possibly be lovers.

Looking at the rest of the company about the table, she saw the couple she had witnessed earlier, and immediately a warmth recalled itself into her loins. The man seemed to feel her gaze and looked in her direction. He winked. Mildred flushed to the roots of her hair and quickly looked down at her soup.

Good heavens. She supposed she ought not feel chagrinned, but the more outlandish aspects of the château required some acclimating. Despite her discomfort, she found herself more eager than ever to engage in the château's purpose. With a life of married ennui before her, she ought to soak in what Château Follet offered.

"Forgive me for introducing myself," the man to her right said, "though we do dispense with the customary formalities here at Château Follet."

"Indeed? I would not have guessed," Mildred replied.

The man smiled in seeming appreciation. "Charming. I must have your name?"

"Miss, er, Abbey."

"Miss Abbey, a pleasure. I am the Viscount Devon."

"Pleased to meet you, my lord."

"You are new to me. Is this your first time?"

"Yes."

With interest, he turned his body farther toward her. "Then you are in for quite a delight."

Happy to have someone to talk to and hopeful that she would

not have to spend the evening in her own company, she gave him her most winning smile. Though barely average in height, Lord Devon was quite attractive with his golden locks and bright blue eyes.

He looked to see who sat to her left. It was a woman of striking beauty. Mildred expected he would attempt to make the acquaintance of the woman beside her, but he returned his gaze to her.

"Are you here with someone?" he asked.

"No, I am alone."

"As am I."

The palpitation of her heart quickened. Could this debonair man—a Viscount, if he gave his name truthfully—possibly be interested in her?

Just then, she thought she heard a familiar baritone come from the doors behind her. A mouse coming face to face with a hawk could not have felt more ill.

"Marguerite, your pardon for my late arrival. I am most sorry," the gentleman said.

"La, Andre! You are *not* sorry for being tardy."

"I *am* sorry I was thrown from my horse, which was the cause of my delay."

Mildred did not hear Madame Follet's response. The blood had drained from her.

It could not be. It could not be!

She wanted to turn and look to confirm her fears, but she could not risk revealing herself.

"Miss Abbey, are you well?" Devon asked. "Forgive me, but you look pale of a sudden."

As she faced Devon, she discerned that the man she suspected to be Alastair stood near the other end of the table, where Madame sat.

"The soup does not agree with me, I think," she whispered.

"But you have hardly touched it."

"I was unsure if you would come," Madame said, "but I have saved you a seat for dinner."

From the corner of her eye, she saw the man rounding the

table. She recognized the build, the height, the jet-black hair. Dear heavens, it was Alastair!

In a panic, she bent down behind the table as if she had dropped something.

"Miss Abbey?" Devon inquired, bending down as well.

"I think one of my earrings fell," she said, pretending to look about the floor.

"They are both of them in your ears."

She blinked several times, her mind in a whir. "Oh, well, thank you."

Realizing she could not spend the dinner beneath the table, she sat back up, holding her napkin before her face and keeping herself angled toward her end of the table. Her heart raced. What was she to do? She could not keep her napkin at her face the entire dinner. This was dreadful! She had to find a way to leave.

"I forgot my—my—something—in my chambers," she murmured as she rose.

She would not be able to excuse herself to the hostess but hoped Madame Follet would forgive her later. Alastair sat across the table near the other end. If she turned to her right and went through the set of doors nearest to her, he would not glimpse her face.

Holding the napkin in front of her still, she made for the egress—and walked straight into a maid carrying a tureen of gravy. The contents splashed down the front of Mildred's gown.

"Oh, miss, I'm terribly sorry!" the maid cried.

"Miss Abbey!" Lord Devon cried, coming to her aid.

One of the other gentlemen had approached to help with picking up the tureen.

"I'm quite all right," Mildred mumbled, conscious that half the table had risen to look her way. She reached down for the napkin she had dropped.

Lord Devon took her elbow. "Are you certain—"

"Yes, yes, I am fine," she assured him before stepping into a puddle of gravy in her haste to flee.

Once outside the dining hall, she hurried down the corridor, but her legs had begun to shake with violence. She slipped into an empty but lighted parlor. Closing the door behind her, she leaned against it and sank to the floor.

It was Alastair. She knew his voice, and Madame had called him by name. She was not at all surprised that he would be known to Madame, but how was it he should be here the very same evening as her? And what was she to do now that he was?

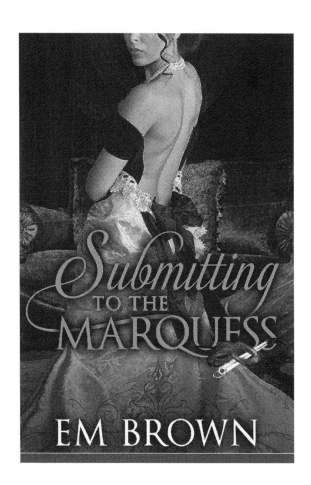

Read on for more…

Episode One:

MASTER
VS.
Mistress

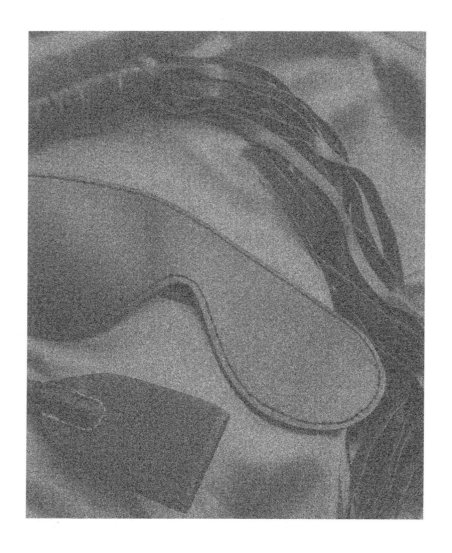

Episode One:

‟**T**HIS IS A DILEMMA FOR the mind of Solomon,” said Madame Joan Devereux, proprietress of the Inn of the Red Chrysanthemum, as she took a sip of her cordial and settled further into her sofa. “Alas, I am no King Solomon.”

Charles glanced over his shoulder at the fair young woman— the babe in need of splitting—standing in shadow in the back of the room with her eyes downcast and her hands clasped demurely before her in perfect submission. Through her thin chemise, he could see hints of her garters and the form of two slender legs. With her thick eyelashes, charming little nose, and soft flaxen curls cascading to breasts that required no stays for lift, she had caught the attention of nearly every patron within the inn Madame Devereux maintained for members to indulge their most taboo proclivities.

Another woman, with reddish hair coiffed starkly from her face, stood an arm’s length from Charles and protested to Madame Devereux, “I approached her first.”

“A happenstance facilitated by distance,” Charles replied with a polite bow.

The redhead did not look at him, but he sensed he had irked her. He regretted the antagonism of his first exchange with Mistress Scarlet, as she was known at the establishment, but he saw an opportunity worthy of risk.

"Regardless, the rule here is that the master or mistress with senior standing may have their choice among the neophytes," Mistress Scarlet said. "Perhaps Master…"

"Gallant. Charles Gallant."

He bowed once more, but his civility failed to encourage a more friendly reception from her. Even from a distance, he had discerned her aloofness. But if she had desired no one to approach her, she should have attempted less provocative attire. Befitting her sobriquet, she wore stays of red silk, edged in black with black ribbons. The color and shape of her stays might have been a fashion from the previous century. The garment pressed her breasts tightly to her body and barely came above the nipples. She wore a shift and stockings, but no petticoats, and had completed her ensemble with shoes and a loosely draped banyan of the same vibrant red as her stays.

With his hat and gloves still in hand, his coat buttoned, and his cravat perfectly tied, Charles felt overdressed for the establishment.

"Perhaps *he* is unaware of the rules we have instituted," Mistress Scarlet finished.

"*I* instituted," Madame Devereux clarified.

Despite the dim lighting afforded by the few candles about the drawing room, Charles could see the color in Mistress Scarlet heighten. She had always been prone to blushing, he recalled. He found it becoming. It would be even more becoming if he were the cause of her flush. His groin tightened at the thought.

"Yes, Madam," Mistress Scarlet acknowledged with lowered eyes.

It was a small movement, but it gave him hope.

"If seniority decides," he said, "I doubt there is a member who has more years than I."

Surprised, she examined him more closely before turning back to Madame Devereux with raised brows.

Madame Devereux finished her drink. "Yes. You were a patron shortly after the inn had been renamed the Red Chrysanthemum"

"I was one of your first patrons."

"But how long has his leave of absence lasted?" Mistress Scarlet objected. "I have not seen him here in my time."

Charles did not correct her. She had seen him before, during her first year as a patron of the Inn. She had merely forgotten. He did not fault her for it. He knew her then as Miss Margaret Barlow, and at the time, she had been quite immersed with a selfish cad named Damien.

"I have the more recent, uninterrupted tenure," Mistress Scarlet added.

Madame Devereux sighed. "I never thought to have such a predicament or that 'seniority' required a definition."

"A simple refinement, Madame. With all due respect to Master Gallant's past patronage, I do not think anyone would fault you for granting senior standing to one who has demonstrated a more current loyalty?"

Madame Devereux looked from one to another, then to the young woman behind them. "Miss Lily, come forth."

Eyes still downcast, Miss Lily took a step forward.

"Closer. You may look at me, *ma cherie*. Ah, yes, you are quite the lovely thing. I can see why they should both desire you. What a lucky girl you are. Tell me, who would you prefer? Mistress Scarlet or Master Gallant?"

The young woman's eyes widened. "It is not my place to choose, my lady."

"We have ourselves an unusual situation. You may assist in its resolution."

Mistress Scarlet stiffened. Charles guessed she felt a little betrayed by Madame Devereux, but she could not defy the proprietress and turned to smile at Miss Lily. Miss Lily looked first to Mistress Scarlet, then to Charles. He knew himself to be handsome in form and countenance and instantly caught the brightening of appreciation in her doe-like eyes.

"I know not, my lady..." Miss Lily demurred, returning her gaze to her hands.

"It is too difficult to ask her to form a judgment on appearance alone," he offered. "Appearances offer little prospective on the experience to be had. May I suggest that we aid her decision with samples of what she may enjoy?"

Mistress Scarlet narrowed her eyes at him. Her skepticism of him was much higher than he anticipated, but it did not daunt him.

"We could, each of us, have a turn with Miss Lily, for no more than, say, an hour each," he continued. "At the conclusion, Miss Lily will have much better information with which to make a decision. Whomever Miss Lily chooses may then claim their heart's desire for the appointed sennight."

"An inspired thought, Charles!" Madame Devereux praised.

Mistress Scarlet frowned and eyed the quality of his cravat, the tailoring of his coat, and the shine of his boots. "Master Gallant appears to be a gentleman of means. I know nothing of his character, and I mean no impertinence, but what if he were to offer Miss Lily a monetary enticement that I could not match?"

No impertinence, he echoed to himself. The devil she didn't. But she had provided him the opening he needed.

"I invite Mistress Scarlet to bear witness," he said.

She stared at him, disbelieving, then pursed her lips in displeasure. The image of those lips wrapped about his cock flashed through his mind.

He turned his attention to Madame Devereux, a safer subject. "But I do not require the same courtesy. Your trust in her is sufficient for me."

Out of fairness or to prevent him from claiming too much gallantry, Mistress Scarlet responded, "We should both of us submit to the same rules. But it is quite possible that, at the end of this little trial, Miss Lily remains undecided."

"I am confident my abilities will not fail to persuade."

His arrogance provoked the answer he needed from Mistress Scarlet. Her hazel eyes hardened.

"Very well. I accept this proposal."

"One hour each with a respite for Miss Lily in between. The winner is awarded the maiden of his choice."

"Or *her* choice."

Charles suppressed a smile. He rarely adopted this much hauteur, but he had Mistress Scarlet—Miss Greta, as he preferred—right where he wished. His first visit back to the Inn had exceeded all expectation.

GRETA WRESTLED UNSUCCESSFULLY WITH HER indignation as she led Master Gallant and Miss Lily to the room Madame Devereux had appointed for their purpose. Who the devil was this man attempting to usurp her seniority and why had Madame Devereux obliged him? Had he bribed Madame? Did they share some manner of history? Seven years was a long time, Greta supposed. He looked vaguely familiar to her, but she had ceased attending to his sex for some time.

"Our chamber," Greta said as she opened the door to a modest room lit by a few candelabras and a small flame from the hearth.

"Little has changed since last I was here," observed Master Gallant.

Feeling territorial, she found his remark irritating. She watched him as he took a closer look at the apparatus and instruments of pain and pleasure adorning the room. The Inn of the Red Chrysanthemum attracted a variety of members, and Master Gallant had the appearance and manners of polite society. With his smartly tailored clothes and handsome features, he could want for little. She had nothing comparable to his trappings. The Inn was the only place she felt she was in command, the only place she could equal anyone who passed its threshold. And she had, through her constant patronage, granting every request of Madame Devereux so that she might not be relieved of her membership to the Inn when she could not afford its dues, earned the right to certain privileges. Tonight that privilege was Miss Lily.

But Charles Gallant would deprive her of that privilege.

Few newcomers were willing to submit to one of their own sex. Miss Lily had indicated she would accept a Mistress or a Master. With his poetic wind-swept hair, long lashes fringing crystalline eyes, and disarming smile, he would have had no shortage of women willing to offer their bodies for his pleasure. It almost seemed as if he insisted on having Miss Lily merely to provoke *her*.

He removed a flogger from the wall and splayed the tails over his palm. Greta could not help but notice his hands. Fine, capable hands. He slid the tails through his fingers and whipped them through the air.

"We should ascertain if Miss Lily has any prohibitions," he said.

"I know the protocol," Greta snapped and instantly regretted her display of vexation. She had no wish to reveal how much he could irritate her. It showed a loss of command and could not aid her efforts to attract Miss Lily.

"Forgive my impertinence," he said, replacing the flogger. "I had no desire to insult you."

His gracious response surprised and unsettled her. She appreciated his willingness to shoulder the blame, but she would rather he did not appear in a more favorable light to Miss Lily.

"Miss Lily," Greta said with a gentleness she hoped would overcome her earlier harshness, "what limits do you wish to make known to us?"

"I have none, Mistress," Miss Lily replied.

"None? There is no device that you disdain? Or a part of your body you wish untouched?"

"I am yours to do as you will, Mistress."

Greta groaned inwardly at the possibilities and with chagrin at the prospect of losing such a gem to Master Gallant.

"Have you had a Master or a Mistress before?" Gallant asked.

"I was the favored pet of a baron and his wife, Master."

"For how long?"

"A sixmonth."

"Had you submitted to others before?"

Eager to proceed, Greta raised her brows at all the questioning.

"A stable boy was my first before the baron and baroness, Master."

"And what was the extent of your submission? Did your master or mistress possess one of these or their like?"

He stood between a pillory and a cross with shackles dangling from the ends. Miss Lily shook her head. He walked over to her and gently lifted her chin to meet her gaze. He spoke as if to a child.

"Your experience, Miss Lily, is limited, I think."

"But I wish to—to explore my limits, Master."

She seemed to hold her breath awaiting his response. He released her.

"Very well. Do you have a safety word that you prefer? When you use it, we will understand you to have reached a limit."

"I like 'flowers.'"

"One syllable is best," Greta said.

Miss Lily said nothing. Greta sighed. She was off to a poor start. While her recommendation demonstrated her knowledge, it also made her sound insensitive.

"How about 'rose'?" Gallant suggested.

"If it please you, Master."

"Does it please *you*?"

Miss Lily appeared perplexed.

"You are the proprietor of the safety word. We cannot utter it for you. Thus, it must be one you are willing to use."

"I shall, Master."

"Are you certain? You must not have any qualms in using it."

"I am certain, Master."

"Do you always engage your subjects in such lengthy interrogations?" Greta asked. "I think we ought not keep Miss Lily waiting further."

He turned to stare at her. "Appearances, or verbal representations of them, are not always what they seem."

His tone—no, his look—intimated a second meaning to his words, as if he were referring to her instead of Miss Lily. What a trying man, Greta thought.

"Miss Lily has a long evening ahead of her," she replied.

"Yes," he said more cheerfully, "it shall be long but memorable."

"Miss Lily, do you prefer that I or Master Gallant should begin?"

Again, Miss Lily was at a loss. The poor creature was truly indecisive, Greta decided.

"Ladies first," Gallant said with a sweep of the arm.

Greta shook her head to herself. If they were in a ballroom or soiree of sorts, he would no doubt have the place charmed. She could not deny his manners sounded sincere and not affected. His eyes had a boyish gleam that could not be overlooked.

Shaking herself to attention, she strode over to where the hand-held implements lined the wall and selected for herself a crop. She slid off her banyan and hung it on a coat rack stand.

"Let my hour begin," she declared.

CHARLES SWALLOWED AN OATH. HIS cock had perked at the first sight of Mistress Scarlet, his reaction differing none from his experience four years ago when she was as shy and uncertain as Miss Lily. He had removed himself from the Inn because his attraction to her had only grown, and he saw no purpose in torturing himself with temptation that he could not satisfy. When he had heard that she was no longer with Damien and unattached to another Master, he could not allow the opportunity to pass him by.

Finding her a Mistress, however, had thrown a decided wrench to his plans. He had had little doubt that he could persuade her to take him on for a Master and that he could prove more capable than Damien, but if she had converted to a Mistress, his order had become much more difficult. If not impossible. Madame Devereux had informed him that Miss Greta had taken no Master after Damien and, for the past year, confined herself to members of the fair sex.

But absurd challenges did not daunt Charles. To possess Miss Greta, he would risk failure over and over.

He watched Miss Greta—Mistress Scarlet—saunter over to Miss Lily. Mistress Scarlet possessed a fullness to her body that he preferred over the willowy Miss Lily, but both women were enticing, and the vision of the two together was almost more than his senses could bear. He unbuttoned and removed his coat. He would need more range of motion for his turn. For now, he needed relief from the growing heat of his own body.

Mistress Scarlet circled Miss Lily, admiring the qualities of the latter, and caressed the length of one arm with the riding crop.

"What a beauty you are, Miss Lily."

"Thank you, Mistress."

"I have a few rules of my own," Mistress Scarlet informed, her voice a buttery mezzo-soprano. "First, you will not speak unless spoken to. Second, you will thank me for everything I do to you, be it pleasurable or painful. And third, you are not to spend until I grant you permission. Disobedience will be severely punished. Do you understand?"

"Yes, Mistress."

"Good."

Charles swallowed with difficulty. He grabbed a simple wooden chair and sat down. Seated, his erection would be less obvious.

"Disrobe for me," Mistress Scarlet instructed.

Miss Lily slid her chemise down, revealing her breasts, a flat abdomen, and lean thighs. The garment pooled at her feet.

"Ah, you have trimmed yourself," Mistress Scarlet noted, brushing two fingers along the patch of hair between Miss Lily's legs. She took a step back. "Simply lovely. I wonder that your baron and baroness could relinquish such a treasure. Were you disobedient?"

"No, Mistress."

"Ungrateful?"

"No, Mistress."

"Did you no longer enjoy being their 'pet'?"

"No, Mistress, but I think I no longer amused them and they found another."

Mistress Scarlet hesitated. Charles caught a flash of pain in her eyes, but it was momentary.

"Their loss is my gain," the Mistress said, recovering. "Clasp your hands behind your head."

She reached out and tugged an already stiff nipple. Lowering herself, she licked the little rosebud. Charles refrained from gaping at the extension of her tongue and crossed his leg on top of the other. Miss Lily shivered, then moaned as Mistress Scarlet suckled the nipple, drawing it deep into her mouth.

"Thank you, Mistress," Miss Lily said when Mistress Scarlet withdrew.

Lightly, Mistress Scarlet tapped the same breast with her crop. "Tell me, how well do you tolerate pain?"

"Well, I think, Mistress."

Mistress Scarlet whipped the crop against the side of the breast. Miss Lily inhaled sharply.

"Thank you, Mistress," Mistress Scarlet reminded her.

"Thank you, Mistress."

"Do not forget again."

"Yes, Mistress."

She brought the crop to the breast once more, harder this time, making the orb wobble. Miss Lily grunted.

"Thank you, Mistress."

"Do not lower your arms."

Mistress Scarlet struck the nipple this time. Miss Lily cried out. Mistress Scarlet struck the other. Another cry.

Setting aside the crop, Mistress Scarlet took a nipple in each hand and rolled them between her thumbs and forefingers.

"Such pretty rosebuds. I think a little decoration is in order."

Walking to the sideboard, she opened a drawer and pulled out a pair of silver clamps attached to metal balls. Charles wanted to ask if there were smaller clamps for Miss Lily to begin with, but it was not his place to interject. Mistress Scarlet affixed a clamp to Miss Lily's nipple, then allowed the metal ball to drop. Miss Lily shrieked as the weight pulled her nipple down.

"The pain will dissipate."

But Miss Lily was having a tough time. She whimpered and breathed through clenched teeth. Mistress Scarlet affixed the other clamp. Miss Lily screamed once more and nearly doubled over.

Charles could not refrain. "Do you recall your safety word, Miss Lily?"

Mistress Scarlet glared at him. "Miss Lily stated that she wished to explore her limits."

She turned to Miss Lily and stroked the young woman's cheek.

"The greater the pain, the greater the pleasure, my pet."

"Yes, Mistress," Miss Lily replied, her voice an octave higher.

"You forgot my second rule."

"Thank you, Mistress!"

"Too late."

Taking the small chain from which the ball dangled, she jerked the clamp off. Charles was sure the screech that followed could be heard across town. He rose to his feet when Miss Lily fell to her knees. What the devil was Mistress Scarlet about? She could not possibly win if she carried on in such fashion.

As if struck by the same thought or chastened by Miss Lily's sobs, Mistress Scarlet removed the other clamp gently and assisted Miss Lily back to her feet. Retrieving the crop, Mistress Scarlet inserted it between Miss Lily's thighs and brushed it along her folds. After a length of time, Miss Lily recovered from the painful assault to her nipples and responded to the fondling. She moaned and purred. Charles settled back into his chair.

"My, we are a wanton creature, are we not?" Mistress Scarlet asked. She tweaked a nipple. "Answer me!"

"Yes, Mistress!"

"How wanton?"

"Extremely wanton, Mistress."

"Wanton enough to beg?"

"Yes, Mistress."

She quickened her ministrations. "Do you wish to spend upon my crop?"

"Yes, Mistress."

"Then beg for it. Beg to spend upon my crop."

"Please, Mistress, I wish to spend upon your crop."

"Louder."

"Please, Mistress, I wish to spend upon your crop!"

"More."

"Please, I beg of you, permit me to spend. Please, Mistress!"

Mistress Scarlet agitated the crop against Miss Lily in short, fast strokes. Seeing Miss Lily in the throes of carnal delight, her skin flush, her lips pouting, her eyelashes fluttering, Charles felt his cock stretch painfully against his trousers.

"Permission granted."

A few minutes later, Miss Lily emitted a pitched groan and her body trembled. Mistress Scarlet slowed the crop and withdrew it glistening from the nectar of Miss Lily's desire. Charles adjusted the crotch of his trousers. There was nothing more titillating than a woman in orgasm. But Mistress Scarlet showed no signs of being aroused. He wondered that she had allowed Miss Lily to spend before she herself had been satisfied. Perhaps she thought it a better strategy to grant Miss Lily as much pleasure as possible to win the match.

"Thank you, Mistress."

Mistress Scarlet held the crop before Miss Lily. "Clean it."

Dutifully, Miss Lily licked and sucked at the implement. This time Charles put his focus on Mistress Scarlet, looking for indications of lust. She had an intense look in her gaze, but her desire was not obvious. He supposed his presence might have discomforted her, but she seemed ensconced in her own world.

"You may lie upon the bed, Miss Lily."

While Miss Lily stretched herself upon the simple four-post bed, Mistress Scarlet returned the crop and retrieved a long phallus made of lacquered wood.

"Spread your legs."

From where he sat, Charles had an unobstructed view of Miss Lily's cunnie, swollen and wet from the earlier attention. He wondered if he would have a chance at a similar view of Mistress Scarlet. The thought made the heat churn in his loins.

Mistress Scarlet worked the phallus into Miss Lily, who moaned her pleasure.

"Thank you, Mistress."

Mistress Scarlet went to one of the candelabras upon the wall and removed a candle, carrying it carefully back to the bed so that the flame would not extinguish. Holding it above the torso of Miss Lily, she tilted the candle. A large drop of the melted wax fell. Miss Lily let out a sharp cry. Charles shook his head. He would have paused to ensure that Miss Lily remembered her safety word first.

"As lovely a vision as a *rose*," he commented.

Mistress Scarlet frowned at him. "I would prefer you did not disturb *my* time with Miss Lily."

He clenched a hand. He had a great urge to splay her across his lap and spank her.

Mistress Scarlet smoothed the hair from Miss Lily's forehead. "You are lovely, my pet, truly lovely."

The candle tilted once more. The wax seared Miss Lily upon the abdomen.

"Thank you, Mistress," she mewed after a haggard scream.

"Very good. You may pleasure yourself."

Miss Lily reached a tentative hand between her thighs.

"You wish to spend again, do you not?"

"Yes, Mistress."

Miss Lily brushed her fingers against the rosy nub between her nether lips.

Mistress Scarlet cupped a breast, squeezed it, then adorned it with a drop of molten wax.

"You may spend as you wish, my pet."

Miss Lily quickened her fingers—out of desire or a need to put an end to the tortuous wax, Charles was unsure. He doubted Mistress Scarlet knew either, though it was her responsibility to know.

"What a sight you are," Mistress Scarlet continued. "Naked but for your stockings, a cock secure in your quim, pleasuring yourself. You are a depraved little wench, are you not?"

"Yes, Mistress."

"A dirty little whore."

"Yes, Mistress."

Miss Lily fondled herself with increasing fury as Mistress Scarlet, like an artist applying paint to canvass, continued to drip the candle with one hand while kneading a breast with the other. Miss Lily arched herself into her own hand, panting harder and harder. Lowering herself, Mistress Scarlet took a nipple in her mouth, licking, biting, and sucking. The attention pushed Miss Lily over the edge. She cried out as her body jerked. When the last of the tremors had subsided and her breathing took on a more regular cadence, Miss Lily opened her eyes.

"Thank you, Mistress."

Mistress Scarlet looked over the hardened wax upon the young woman's body. "You have done well, my pet."

Miss Lily smiled wanly.

Mistress Scarlet turned to Charles. "Your turn, Master Gallant."

GRETA SMIRKED AT THE ERECTION protruding against the flap of his trousers. Men were so easily aroused. If it had been him instead of Miss Lily, would he have lasted half an hour? she wondered. Taking another chair, she situated herself against the wall and watched as he stood and unbuttoned his waistcoat. Though it was possible Miss Lily might have a small preference for his sex over her own, Greta felt confident. She had allowed Miss Lily to spend twice without requiring much effort on the part of Miss Lily to earn the privilege. She had removed the phallus from Miss Lily but left the wax. He could take his time and remove it or leave it be, a reminder of where Mistress Scarlet had tread.

He pried a piece of congealed wax off her breast and gently blew upon the exposed flesh. He cleared her breasts of the candlewax but allowed the other splatters to remain.

"Would you like a cordial, Miss Lily?" he asked.

Miss Lily nodded.

From the sideboard, he poured her a glass. Miss Lily sat up and sipped the drink.

"Shall I order tea?" Greta asked. "I was under the impression we were here to gratify one's concupiscence or do you wish to pamper the girl more?"

He looked at her calmly. "It can be one and the same."

Greta folded her arms. *Ridiculous.* What sort of Master was this Charles Gallant?

Setting aside the now empty glass, he rummaged through the sideboard and pulled out two coils of rope. The shorter one he used to tie Miss Lily's wrists together behind her back. The longer one he wound across her chest and around the base of each breast, making the orbs protrude further from the body. The effect was surprisingly alluring, drawing more attention to the breasts, and decorating the bosom the way lace might enhance a garment.

"When you were with the baron and baroness, what did you enjoy most?" Gallant asked.

"To be spanked, Master."

Greta frowned. She had not thought to address Miss Lily's rump.

"Were you spanked often?"

"Not as often as I would have wished, Master."

Grasping the rope binding her breasts, he pulled her off the bed. He turned her around and assessed her derriere.

"You have a delightful arse, Miss Lily."

A skinny one, Greta thought to herself.

"It ought be spanked," Gallant remarked.

Lightly, he traced their contours with his hand, then smacked the side of one, making it quiver.

"Mmmm. Thank you, Master."

"If you desire more, you must earn it."

"Yes, Master."

He slid his hand between her thighs, feeling her dampness. "Mistress Scarlet has aroused you well."

"Yes, Master."

He undid her garters. Her stockings slid down her legs. Kneeling, he helped her step from them, then caressed the length of one leg from her ankle, up a calf, along the thigh, and past the hip. Miss Lily shivered.

"Cold?" he asked.

"Your touch is warm, Master—and pleasant."

Standing behind her, he gripped her at the waist. "You require more flesh upon you. One could toss you about too easily, Miss Lily."

He turned her toward a wall where a tall mirror hung. "Nonetheless, you are quite fetching, to the eye and touch."

She looked into the mirror and watched as his hands went up her torso and cupped her tender breasts.

"These beauties have suffered a lovely abuse. If you please me, perhaps I shall pass over them and grant them a reprieve."

He threaded his hand through her hair and pulled, forcing her chin up. "I do recommend you please me, Miss Lily."

As he held her close to him, his free hand trailed down to her abdomen. Sliding his fingers between her thighs, he fondled her. Miss Lilly purred. Greta bit upon her lower lip. She had not been such a close witness to another's performance since her days with Damien. She did not like how the sight of Master Gallant's hands upon Miss Lily stirred a familiar sensation.

"How may I please you?" Miss Lily asked between moans.

He ceased his fondling and yanked her hair. Her head fell against his broad shoulder.

"Master!" she quickly added.

Still holding her in place, he resumed his ministrations. "How would you like to please me, Miss Lily?"

"It would please me to suck your cock, Master."

How trite, Greta thought. Damien enjoyed seeing his cock wrapped between a pair of lips, and she had willingly taken him into her mouth several times, begging at times to have a taste of him. She had enjoyed having his thickness in her mouth. Though one might consider such an act debasing, she experienced a thrill for it was no small matter for a man to submit his most vulnerable organ in such a fashion. His cock had been hers to pleasure and cherish.

Till he chose to share it.

Pushing away the unwanted memory, Greta sighed as if bored. She hoped she would not have to observe Miss Lily upon her knees, though she was a little curious to see what sort of cock Master Gallant possessed.

By now he had Miss Lily squirming against him.

"Please, may I suck your cock, Master?" Miss Lily panted. "*Please.*"

"You like the taste of cock-meat, do you?"

"Yes, Master. Please let me taste you. Please."

Her pleas grew more urgent as he quickened his rubbing,

advancing her impending climax. Greta shifted in her seat. It had been some time since she had spent at the hand of another, instead of her own. Perhaps she should not have confined herself to such a lengthy abstinence....

"Please...I wish...for your...cock."

"Such melodic begging," he said. "You have pleased me, Miss Lily."

He removed his hand and stepped away from her. Miss Lily had been near to spending and groaned at the sudden deprivation. Greta, too, inhaled sharply. If Miss Lily had pleased him, why had he stopped?

"Your patience shall be rewarded," he replied.

Pressing upon her back, he bent Miss Lily over the bed. Her rump rounded the edge of the bed. After caressing her buttocks with his gaze, he went over and retrieved the nine-tails he had handled earlier.

"Do you recall your safety word?"

"Rose," Miss Lily answered.

He swung the tails lightly against her arse. The moisture from her arousal was beginning to ebb down her inner thighs.

"Count for me, Miss Lily."

He slapped the tails upon a buttock. Her body jerked, mostly in surprise, for he had not applied the flogger too harshly.

"One, Master."

He repeated the blow upon the other buttock.

"Two, Master."

Increasing his force slightly, he aimed the tails square upon both cheeks.

"Three, Master!"

"Your ass quivers deliciously, Miss Lily."

Greta swallowed. His skill with the flogger was evident. Damien, too, had had command of the implement.

Master Gallant slid his hand past her buttocks and played with her once more. Miss Lily had her face turned to the side, and Greta could see the pleasure in her flushed cheeks and pursed lips. He pulled back his hand and lashed at her backside. Miss Lily gasped, then moaned.

"My count, Miss Lily," he reminded her.

"Four, Master!"

He whipped her rump thrice in succession. Miss Lily was upon her toes as if attempting to scramble away.

"Five, six, seven! Master."

He rewarded her with more fondling. Greta felt the tug between her legs. She clenched her thighs. Perhaps she should have gone second. Now her budding frustration would have no outlet. Even if Miss Lily chose her the winner, the young woman was likely done for the evening.

"Eight, Master!"

Miss Lily's arse blushed from the attention, yet Greta knew, from the manner in which he had snapped the tails through the air earlier, that the blows were but a fraction of what Master Gallant was capable of. She wondered how much of it she herself could have withstood. Though her tolerance may have waned over the years, she wagered she could bear more than Miss Lily, especially if she were as aroused as the young woman. The pleasure betwixt the pain would have enabled her to endure.

"Ohhhhh, Master, may I…nine!"

Despite the diminishing flame in the fireplace, Greta felt increasingly warm from the familiar sound of tails slapping against flesh.

"Ten, Master!"

Her arse glowed an angry red from the last strike. Master Gallant agitated his hand against Miss Lily's most intimate parts. Greta wondered that his hand did not cramp from the exertion.

"Master, Master!"

Her cries of delight reached a fevered pitch. He withdrew his hand and applied another wallop with the flogger. Greta swallowed a grunt, wanting him to finish, to allow Miss Lily to spend, for her own sake as well as Miss Lily's.

"Eleven, Master, twelve!"

Greta nearly felt the sting in her own arse. Desire pooled low and hot in her loins. Master Gallant tossed the flogger onto the bed and began leisurely unbuttoning his fall. She could not tear her gaze from his crotch. He pulled out his stiff member. She felt a tug in her cunnie. He took a step toward and Miss Lily and pointed his cock between her thighs. With his boot, he spread her legs wider. And then he took her. Greta felt a stab of envy as his cock disappeared from view. Her own cunnie pulsed, the emptiness palpable.

Miss Lily groaned. Her eyes were closed as she took the length of him inside of her. Gently he pushed himself until the whole of his shaft was buried and her rump was pressed firmly against the hairs of his pelvis. He remained still, allowing her time to adjust to the fullness, then slowly withdrew. Miss Lily moaned. He pushed himself in again. She moaned loader. He withdrew and thrust himself deeper this time, the muscles of his arse flexing. She twitched. He increased his pace. Having been urged to the brink many times before, Miss Lily did not require long before she let out a cry and began convulsing about his cock.

Greta watched, her own cunnie throbbing, the wetness grown, wishing she could frig herself in solitude. She knew better than to fool herself into thinking that mere abstinence caused her current state of arousal, her desire for release. She could not deny that Master Gallant had played a part in exciting those old familiar feelings. But she would be damned if she allowed him to know it.

He had slowed his thrusting in response to Miss Lily's paroxysm but did not stop. Greta could see he had not spent. He increased his pace and the force of his movements. Miss Lily groaned. As he slammed into her limp body, he chanced to look at Greta. His stare pierced hers and struck a scorching blow deep within her womanhood. She almost fancied—or was it wishful thinking— that he intended to fuck *her* instead of Miss Lily.

Her pulse quickening even more, Greta tried to tear her gaze away, but his rhythmic pummeling mesmerized. The heat within her was more uncomfortable than the pains of hunger, and she suspected that even when she had the opportunity to bring herself to spend, the result would not be as fulfilling.

Despite her fatigue, Miss Lily became excited once again. Gallant reached a hand around her hip and began fondling her from the front while his cock continued its assault from the rear. The dual stimulation had Miss Lily crying and groaning. Greta flexed the muscles of her cunnie, attempting some modicum of relief. She hoped Miss Lily would spend soon and put an end to the scene.

With his other hand Gallant held Miss Lily aloft so that he could plunge deeper into her. Greta closed her eyes and imagined what it would feel like to be trapped between the softness of the bed and the hardness of Gallant. Her eyes flew open when Miss Lily's wail filled the room. Miss Lily shuddered violently, her body jerking against Gallant. Her legs buckled, and she would have collapsed to the floor if he did not have her pinned against the bed. After the wave of spasms had crested and broken, he eased himself from her, still hard. Greta could see the moisture glistening down Miss Lily's thighs.

She knew in that moment she had lost.

But more curious to see how Gallant would finish himself than distraught over the realization of her loss, Greta continued to watch him. He lifted Miss Lily, exhausted, onto the bed, then replaced the fall of his trousers over his cock. Greta was surprised—and disappointed—to see his member gone. Why would he deny himself? Did he have more in store for Miss Lily? But surely his time had concluded. Impatient to know, Greta watched him caress the curve of Miss Lily's rump, then the length of her thigh.

"Miss Lily, you failed to request permission to spend," he noted.

Her breathing not yet returned to normalcy, Miss Lily could barely muster a moan.

"But, as my time has expired, we shall have to address that oversight another time."

Greta felt a tingle between her legs at the prospect. While he unloosened the rope about Miss Lily, Greta composed herself. She wanted no hint of the harried state he had stimulated. Straightening her shoulders and ignoring the moisture collected at her cunnie, she rose from her chair. She would be gracious in defeat.

Master Gallant could have Miss Lily. He had earned his victory.

"Congratulations, Master Gallant," Greta said, her chin lifted.

He turned to her in surprise.

"I am sure if the child could speak, she would name you the winner," Greta allowed.

He bowed at her acknowledgment. He said nothing and simply looked at her, his eyes still glowing with lust.

Unnerved by his stare, and not yet free of her own libidinous agitation, she bid him good evening and started for the door. If he intended to frequent the Inn, she might have to halt her own visits until she had more command of her senses around him.

"Where are you headed, Mistress Scarlet?" he asked with a faint edge, as if he were speaking to Miss Lily.

Greta turned around, a little perturbed at his tone. "Your pardon?"

"I have not yet claimed my prize."

Perplexed, she looked over to the bed where Miss Lily continued to lay, perhaps in slumber.

"We agreed that the winner would be awarded the maiden of his choice," he reminded her.

"She is yours," Greta responded.

"Ah, but I have not chosen her."

Greta let out a sigh of irritation. What the deuce did he want? To lord over her with his victory? She met his hard stare with one of her own that he might understand she had no intention of flattering him or indulging him.

"I would have *you*, Miss Greta."

The floor fell from beneath her feet. Her breath stalled. For several moments, she did nothing but blink and stare at him. He, too, seemed to cease breathing as he awaited her response. And for the first time that evening, he appeared a little uncertain.

Was it always her that he had desired? She recalled his vague words earlier in the drawing room—it was true that he had not specified Miss Lily to be the prize—and toyed with the notion that he had intended this outcome all along. After a lengthy silence, a small smile crept to her lips. The blood returned to her. She felt a welcome anticipation at the journey ahead: a sennight with Master Gallant.

THE END

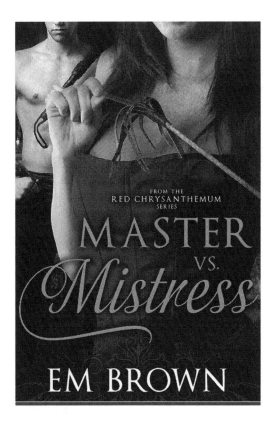

Episode Two:

MASTER
VS.
Mistress

THE CHALLENGE CONTINUES

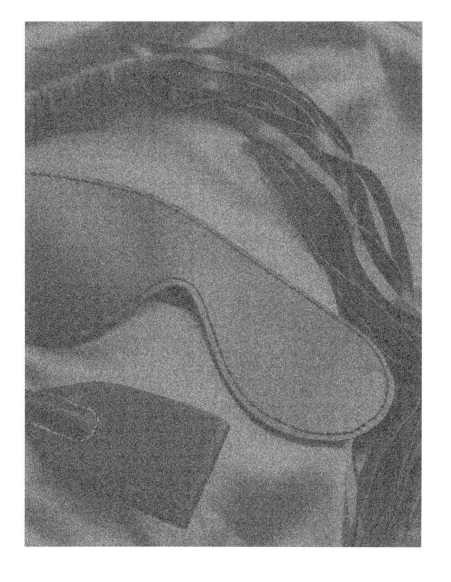

Episode Two:

SITTING WITH HER ARMS CROSSED, one slender leg thrown unladylike over the knee of the other, in purposeful defiance, she gave him her most imposing stare. Despite her petite stature, Miss Greta, in her time as Mistress Scarlet, had acquired a comportment that seemed to lend more height and breadth to her trim frame. Charles Gallant inhaled deeply as he placed his hat and walking stick on a chest of drawers nearby. He could see she had no intention of submitting easily to him. As if to subdue any doubt he might have about *that*, she had worn the costuming of her prior role: a rose red corset from the previous century. Miss Greta had smaller breasts than most women, but the garment pressed the orbs so tightly that they swelled quite nicely toward her elegant collarbone. Her chemise, stockings, a shawl, and pair of red slippers completed her attire. She seemed quite at ease with her state of dress, or lack thereof.

She could have charmed Charles in a peasant blouse and buckskin breeches. He liked her natural beauty and that she did not paint her face as the more fashionable women of society did. The daughter of an apothecary, Miss Greta did not hail from polite society, nor did she seem to aspire to a higher station for herself, though her father had seen to her education in the hopes that she would attract a husband of superior breeding. She had her hair, its hue a cross between red and brown, in a simple, tight coiffure, but he remembered when she used to let her locks cascade down her shoulders. He would see her hair free and flowing before their time was done.

From her chair, she watched in silence as he removed his great coat. Having come from Brooks's, his toilette was more formal than the Red Chrysanthemum required. Not wanting to keep Miss Greta, he had bypassed Madame Devereux's butler in his haste to reach the room where she waited. It was the same room that had served as the stage for his victory, where he had won the right to claim her for a sennight. A fire burned brightly in the hearth, causing the unique furnishings to cast strange shadows. Amidst the chest of drawers, four-post bed, and sideboard, were a wooden cross, stocks, a low and narrow bench, and iron hooks that dangled from the rafters. On the bare walls hung various crops, paddles, whips and canes. The chamber differed greatly from the halls of silk wallpaper and golden candelabras that he had come from, but, despite his hiatus from the Red Chrysanthemum, he felt at home here. His disquiet did not stem from his whereabouts but with Mistress Scarlet.

Miss Greta, he corrected himself, as he removed his gloves. Hell and damnation. If he could not keep her appellation in order, he might as well quit now, his efforts in vain before he had even started. From the corner of his eye, he beheld her uncross her legs and assume her previous position with the opposite leg. Though she continued to stare at him, the language of her body indicated no small amount of *boredom*. No woman had ever found his company dull or wearisome. He moved to the sideboard to pour himself a brandy. Remembering that she enjoyed ratafia, he was tempted to pour her a glass. A part of him wished they were strolling through a park or partaking of sorbet at Gunter's instead of occupying a dim room adorned with implements of pain. He would have enjoyed seeing her smile and hearing the lyrical laughter that had captivated his attention several years ago.

Before Master Damien had ruined her.

Finishing his brandy, he opted not to pour her a glass. She had not merited the courtesy yet. What she merited was a sound punishment for her blatant impudence. And though he would have liked nothing better than to ease her into his company with food, drink and polite conversation, he knew such an approach might present him as too lenient and indulgent, even weak. Traits that did not become one in the dominant role. The lines of distinction had to be clear, and while one could soften from strict to temperate, the reverse was suspect.

He went to stand before her. "I will overlook your display of disrespect this one time for you are unacquainted with my habits, but hereafter, you will show me proper regard. When next we meet, I will find you waiting on your knees, your eyes downcast, till I have given you permission to rise."

Her nostrils flared and her frown deepened. She was ready to hate him. Perhaps she did already. He had to tread carefully. For the better part of two years, Miss Greta had not existed. Only Mistress Scarlet. And, according to Madame Devereux, Mistress Scarlet had limited herself to the fair sex, refusing to take men even as submissive ones. The proprietress had wagered he could not persuade Mistress Scarlet to resume her prior identity of Miss Greta beyond the sennight he had won.

"Fifty guineas that she will return to Mistress Scarlet within days of concluding her time with you," Devereux had said. "As skilled a Master as you are, Charles, I fail to see how you can make a convert of her."

"She would not be the first, nor the only, to switch roles," he had replied. "You have members who oscillate from dominant to submissive with constancy."

"Yes, but I have witnessed Mistress Scarlet for some time now. I have seen how intensely she immerses herself in her role."

Charles had seen Mistress Scarlet's intensity as well in their duel for the hand of Miss Lily but was unconvinced her motivation stemmed from pleasure alone.

"She came to see me when the two of you were finished with Miss Lily and was quite furious at you. I think she wanted me to throw you out."

"I am not particularly proud of the stratagem I employed, but, given what you had told me of her, I saw no other way of convincing her."

"Alas, I think your efforts will be for naught."

"If you are convinced of that, why not make it a hundred guineas?"

Charles was not one to wager such amounts. His income was sufficient to sustain him but not large enough for him to bandy money about on idle causes. But he did not believe Mistress Scarlet was as she appeared to Madame Devereux. His observation lent him to believe that Miss Greta still persisted beneath the domination of the Mistress. And he meant to unearth her.

"Let us enrich the wager," Madame Devereux had returned, and she eyed him as if he were some succulent repast she was to devour. "If I win, I wish for you to become mine, mine to command, to submit to my wishes for a sixmonth."

"An indentured servant?"

"If you will."

"And if I win?"

He fancied Madame Devereux, were she an animal, to be licking her chops in anticipation of feasting.

"Name your prize."

Finished with the reverie of his dialogue with Madame Devereux, Charles placed the full weight of his attention upon the woman before him. Miss Greta might prove more challenging than he had anticipated, but he had every intention of claiming all of her: mind, body, and soul.

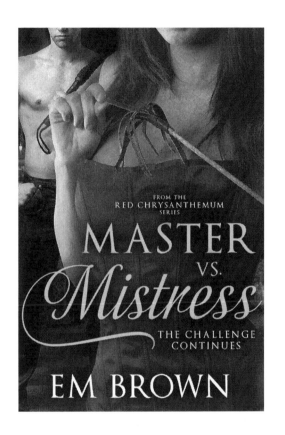

More Wicked Hot Erotic Romance by Em Brown

CAVERN OF PLEASURE SERIES
Mastering the Marchioness
Conquering the Countess
Binding the Baroness
Lord Barclay's Seduction

RED CHRYSANTHEMUM STORIES
Master vs. Mistress
Master vs. Mistress: The Challenge Continues
Seducing the Master
Taking the Temptress
Master vs. Temptress: The Final Submission
A Wedding Night Submission
Punishing Miss Primrose, Parts I - XX

CHATEAU DEBAUCHERY SERIES
Submitting to the Rake
Submitting to Lord Rockwell
Submitting to His Lordship
Submitting to the Baron
Submitting to the Marquess
Submitting for Christmas

OTHER STORIES
Claiming a Pirate

Manufactured by Amazon.ca
Bolton, ON

27163657R00090